As he drew close _____
stopped dead. Th _____

He caught his breath for a second. The last time he'd seen Heather, she'd run from their apartment saying she never wanted to see him again.

"Heather," he said. There was no need to offer his hand. He didn't want to touch that soft skin again. He knew how it felt. For a moment his fingertips almost tingled in remembered response to the satiny texture.

"Hunter," she said.

Barbara McMahon was born and raised in the South, but settled in California after spending a year flying around the world for an international airline. After settling down to raise a family and work for a computer firm, she began writing when her children started school. Now, feeling fortunate in being able to realize a long-held dream of quitting her "day job" and writing full-time, she and her husband have moved to the Sierra Nevada mountains of California, where she finds her desire to write is stronger than ever. With the beauty of the mountains visible from her windows, and the pace of life slower than the hectic San Francisco Bay area where they previously resided, she finds more time than ever to think up stories and characters and share them with others through writing. Barbara loves to hear from readers. You can reach her at P.O. Box 977, Pioneer, CA 95666-0977, U.S.A. Readers can also contact Barbara at her Web site at www.barbaramcmahon.com

WINNING BACK HIS WIFE

Barbara McMahon

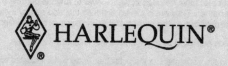

HARLEQUIN®

TORONTO • NEW YORK • LONDON
AMSTERDAM • PARIS • SYDNEY • HAMBURG
STOCKHOLM • ATHENS • TOKYO • MILAN • MADRID
PRAGUE • WARSAW • BUDAPEST • AUCKLAND

ISBN 0-373-03864-X

WINNING BACK HIS WIFE

First North American Publication 2005.

Copyright © 2005 by Barbara McMahon

CHAPTER ONE

HEATHER JACKSON slipped into the conference room late as usual. She hurried to her seat at the long mahogany table and quickly sat, hoping her uncle wouldn't make one of his scathing remarks. Fortunately Saul Jackson was pontificating on some aspect of her cousin Fletcher's latest account and didn't bother to turn his attention to her.

She tried to catch up with what was going on. Sally Myers, sitting next to her, slipped her a note giving a brief recap. She smiled in acknowledgment and began to listen attentively.

A few moments later and Fletcher was off the hook. Her uncle Saul turned his focus to her. She had known her luck had been too good to be true.

"Nice of you to join us, Heather," he said.

She nodded. She was used to his ways. She didn't like to cross him, but had more than once. And undoubtedly would again. He hadn't built one of the largest family-owned advertising businesses in the Pacific Northwest by being Mr. Nice Guy.

He pulled out a sheet from the stack in front of him. "We have a response to the ad copy you sent in for Trails West," he said, holding it up as if exhibit A.

"Did they go for the ad?" Sally asked.

"No."

Heather's heart dropped. She'd been given the account midway into the design stage. She'd picked up where the prelims left off, worked hard, both with drawings and the copy. Adrian Tyler had done the preliminary work on the account, but when his wife had complications during her pregnancy, he'd taken a leave of absence and given Heather all his notes.

She thought she'd captured exactly what the sporting goods company was trying to accomplish with its expansion into the Pacific Northwest. A Denver firm, it had been growing for the last six years—first in the Rockies, then in the California market. Now the company was opening large stores in Seattle, Portland and Yakima simultaneously. She'd really hoped to get the local account for Jackson and Prince.

"At least, not yet," Saul said.

Heather looked up at him. "What does that mean?"

"This is most unusual, but the company wants the top contenders to go one step farther than just providing copy. Apparently the head man wants us to put our money where our mouth is, so to speak."

"And that means what?" she asked again. Did Saul have to be so cryptic?

"According to this, there are five firms in the running. Each firm is to send their account executive on a camping trip to show how much he—" Saul looked at Heather

"—or she, knows about camping and the equipment they sell."

She leaned back in her chair, deflated. "That leaves us out. I haven't a clue about camping."

Fletcher laughed. "Heather's idea of outdoor activity is walking from her car to the mall."

The others around the large table smiled, but no one echoed Fletcher's sentiments. She thought she even caught a hint of sympathy from one of the other junior account executives sitting opposite her.

She frowned at him. "You go, then," Heather snapped at her cousin. Fletcher never let a moment pass if he could give her a dig.

"Hey, it's not my account," he protested.

Had he wished it were? Heather wondered. If the agency signed them, it would be a large account. Her biggest if she nailed it.

"It won't be Heather's account, either, if she doesn't go and demonstrate she's familiar with the products. Trails West wants the account exec to be conversant with all aspects of their products, and able to write glowing copy based on personal experience," Saul finished.

She sighed and looked at her tablet. The last time she'd thought about going hiking had been ten years ago when Hunter had waxed poetic about the beauties of nature, and the high he got pitting his skills against the wild. She knew next to nothing about camping in the wilderness, or hiking mountains.

She doodled on her paper, feeling the familiar sting. She didn't think much about Hunter anymore. She hadn't seen him in ten years. But occasionally something reminded her of him and she mourned for all she'd lost.

Saul put down the paper and looked around the table, stopping at Heather. "I don't think I need to tell any of you the state of the company. We've lost two major accounts in the last four months. Without a few new ones to balance those losses, we could be looking at drastically cutting corners in the near future and maybe laying off personnel."

Heather squirmed in her chair. Was he talking about letting her go? She knew she'd obtained the job because Saul was her uncle and felt a responsibility to his dead brother's family. But only as long as it suited Saul. If she couldn't pull her weight, she'd be gone so fast her head would spin. She'd learned a lot over the last few years. Enough to get this deal? Not unless she somehow became a camping expert overnight.

"I don't know a thing about camping," she protested.

"Learn. The trip starts in two weeks. Bone up on everything you can between now and then and bring us back that account! We're counting on you, Heather. Your mother will be counting on you," Saul said.

That had been unnecessary. Heather knew more than anyone how much her mother counted on her.

He passed her a packet. "Here is the information Trails West sent. Nail the account!"

Heather looked at the stack of papers, they were complete instructions for the camping trip. From the number of sheets, Trails West either planned a mammoth trip, or there was a lot more involved in camping than she suspected.

She'd have to talk to her uncle after the meeting, make him see it would be foolish to expect her to impress some sports nut on her abilities. She resented his putting the welfare of the company on her shoulders. It was his company, not hers. She was merely a minor cog in the wheel. He could send Fletcher. She almost smiled at that picture. Wouldn't her cousin love that? His idea of outdoor activity was watching a football game from the stands.

Reality reared its head. She couldn't afford to lose her job, but she wasn't sure she could do this. Saul couldn't seriously expect her to impress anyone with her camping knowledge.

Granted, her salary was generous, which went a long way in helping with her mother. But it didn't buy her body and soul. She hadn't a clue how to survive in the wilderness. Despite the slur of Fletcher's caustic comment, he was right. She wasn't a very active woman, preferring the quiet pursuits of listening to music or reading to strenuous outdoor activities.

Studying her nails, she tuned out Saul's voice as he moved to a new topic. She loved the fake nails she'd splurged on a few weeks ago. They made her feel successful. No one pinching pennies could afford such extravagances. Glancing at her skirt, she knew the short style suited her long legs. It was only in recent months she felt financially secure enough to indulge herself in small ways. It had been a long haul with exorbitant medical expenses to meet before she felt the least bit secure.

Her mother had made enough negative comments

about her indulgences to give Heather some second thoughts. But the boost to her morale kept her renewing the nails as they grew and searching for bargains in trendy boutiques. She devoted her life to her mother and her job, a few splurges wouldn't hurt.

If she didn't get the Trails West account, however, she could probably kiss future fake nails and trendy skirts goodbye, she thought gloomily. Not to mention the nice apartment she and her mother now lived in, and all the other things that made up their current lifestyle. She wasn't sure she'd get as generous a package at another ad agency—even if she could quickly land a job elsewhere. Sometimes she thought her uncle had given her more chances than anyone else to make up for her father dying and her having to leave college.

"Any questions?" Saul was wrapping up the meeting. Heather looked around and wondered what she'd missed. Nothing as important as what she was going to do about the Trails West account.

As the others left the conference room, Heather lingered. "Saul, we need to talk," she said, catching him before he left.

He looked tired, Heather thought with astonishment. Her bluff, gruff uncle never looked tired. Were things worse than she knew?

"Are you all right?" she asked, drawing closer.

"Of course. What do you wish to talk about?" He rested one hip on the edge of the polished conference table.

"About Trails West. Isn't there someone else you can send? We don't have a prayer if you're depending on me. Fletcher could go. Or Jason," she said desperately, naming one of the men who worked with her on some projects.

He shook his head. "Honey, I know it'll be a challenge, but bone up on camping from books or something. Talk to some of your friends who do that kind of thing. You're strong enough. With all you do with your mother, you have more stamina than you suspect. We need that account." He hesitated a moment, glancing through the opened door, then turned back to her. "We're not doing well. The Trails West account would go a long way to keeping us in the black this year. There are other projects, but none of the magnitude of this single account. Don't think I'm exaggerating when I say the immediate future of the entire company could rest on your securing this account."

Great, just what she didn't need—more responsibility. The fate of the entire company rested on performance on some camping trip? Panic flared. She felt as she had all those years ago when she'd learned her father had crashed his car, killing himself and injuring Heather's mother. She'd responded without hesitation, assuming the burden of her mother's care and comfort while suffering from her own personal loss.

She'd made it through, though some days she'd wondered if she could. Once again she was being put on the spot, being asked to do the impossible. She didn't think she was up to it.

"What about Mother?" she asked, knowing this was a realistic obstacle.

"Susan and I will ask her to stay with us. You'll only be gone a week."

The assignment must truly be important if Aunt Susan was willing to have her mother stay with her for a week. The two women couldn't stand each other. Susan was convinced Amelia could fend for herself and took advantage of Heather. And her mother didn't like anyone who didn't fawn over her. Even Heather knew her mother was more self-centered than most people. But to be confined to a wheelchair for life and battling ill-health had to excuse some of her behavior.

"I'll do my best," she said, resigned to the inevitable.

"I hope it's enough," he said. "We're depending on you, Heather."

Once Heather reached her small office, she closed the door and sat at the tall drafting table near the window that she used for her artwork. She loved designing ads and playing with layouts and styles. Even copy writing could be fun. What she didn't like were meetings with the clients. She had never been good with small talk, and while friendly enough, she preferred her own company to wining and dining prospective clients—who were often total strangers.

Reluctantly she looked in more detail at the information her uncle had given her. The packet gave complete instructions as to what to bring from food and clothing, to sleeping attire and sunscreen. It gave the location of where to meet, the planned itinerary, and how long the trip would last—a full week. It was signed by the director of marketing, Alan Osborne. Would Alan be the one leading the trip? The information sheet simply said a company representative would be present.

Maybe they offered the trip to people in Trails West

who loved this kind of thing. People who relished sports jumped at the chance to work in sporting goods stores. How much more likely would some camping buff be to jump at a chance to get a week's backpacking on company time?

A full week of no showers or baths? Seven days of sleeping on the hard ground, eating who-knew-what out of vacuum-packed aluminum foil, and being 24/7 with strangers. Could she manage to stay the course?

Might as well throw in the towel now, she thought glumly, reading about all the things she was expected to carry. She'd need to be an elephant. And people voluntarily did this for fun?

"And a good time was had by all," she murmured. *"Not."* How would she ever manage seven days in the wilderness with a bunch of strangers—most of whom probably had been camping since they were children?

She glanced at her pretty nails, ran her fingers through her hair. No hair dryer, no salon nearby if she chipped an acrylic nail. She couldn't even expect phone coverage—the area they would be hiking in was remote, no cell service likely. Nothing she was used to.

How could she do it? She was a city girl through and through. When she wanted greenery, she went to the park.

Yet, how could she say no? Her mother depended upon her and her salary. And if Uncle Saul was to be believed, the fate of Jackson and Prince also rested on her performance.

"We who are about to die, salute you," she said valiantly, and began to study the list of equipment and sup-

plies she was to procure prior to meeting the other contenders two weeks from Saturday.

The next Saturday Heather entered the newly opened
Seattle Trails West store. The cavernous space was filled
with items to delight the heart of any sports fan—from
Seahawk logos on T-shirts, sweatshirts, hats, mugs and
key chains, to serious ski equipment. From golf equipment to soccer equipment to a canoe and kayak section,
the store seemed to carry everything. At least she didn't
have to learn to kayak in two weeks, she thought, grateful for small favors.

"Can I help you?" An eager young man came up to
her before she'd finished looking around.

She smiled at him, hoping he wouldn't find her totally
hopeless. "I hope so. Some friends of mine are planning
a camping trip they've talked me into taking. I've never
been, so I need to get some gear. And maybe some hints."

Not wanting anyone to know who she was, or why
she was buying equipment, she'd decided on a cover
story. She felt it only right to purchase her things from
the company she was hoping to woo as a client, but
didn't want anyone knowing ahead of time she hadn't
a clue how to survive in the wilderness.

"I have a list of things they suggested I bring," she
said. She fished out the handwritten list she'd carefully
copied from the information sheet and handed it to the
young man. He scanned it briefly.

"Wow, you want everything. Even new hiking
boots?" He looked doubtful. "You need to break them
in before you begin a long hike. When do you leave?"

"In a couple of weeks," she said vaguely. Employees of Trails West couldn't possibly know of the demands their marketing department put on prospective advertising agencies, could they? Still, she was taking no chances.

"Time enough then to break them in. Let's see, I think we have everything you need." He beamed at her and began walking toward an aisle.

An hour and a half later, and several hundred dollars poorer, Heather was set. As she contemplated the stack of clothing, bedding, cooking utensils, dried food packets and new hiking boots, she wondered how she would even get the things home, much less manage to pack them all in the backpack that balanced on top. She was expected to carry all that for a week? No wonder the instruction sheets urged participants to pack light. Could she manage with one set of clothes, a plate and spoon?

While the happy salesclerk rang up the total, she looked around again. The store was clean, bright and energetic. There were quite a few people shopping or browsing. The grand opening celebration would be in a few weeks. She had hoped to have the account sewn up by now, and devote some attention to a big media push for the event.

However, business already looked brisk.

Looking behind the counter Heather caught her breath. There were two enlarged photos side by side. The founders of Trails West, the caption below them read. Heather's gaze never moved from the one on the left.

Hunter Braddock.

Her heart skipped a beat. She stared at the once familiar face, a sinking sensation flooding through her.

She cleared her throat. "Those are the founders of Trails West?" she asked, though it was clearly stated beneath the portraits.

"Yeah, Hunter Braddock and Trevor McLintock. I've met them both," the young man said proudly. "They came out when this store opened and met all the employees. They'll be back for the grand opening."

"But the firm is headquartered in Denver, right?" she asked, trying to remember what she'd read about the company. Adrian's notes she'd inherited had been primarily devoted to the products and the ways in which the stores differed from other sports establishments. She'd never seen Hunter's name, she knew. She would have recognized it instantly.

She tried to convince herself his being a founder had nothing to do with the account. She couldn't let the past influence the present.

Yet she couldn't stop staring at the photograph. He looked older. Well, of course he would, it had been ten years since she'd seen him. She looked older herself, why should it be a surprise he did as well? Only, somehow he had never changed in her mind. Or in the daydreams she rarely let herself indulge in.

He had obviously done well for himself, if the success of Trails West was anything to go by.

Hunter Braddock. Did he ever think of her?

For a moment she yearned for the carefree months they'd spent together, shattered by the car crash that had killed her father.

If Hunter thought about her, it wouldn't be with longing, she knew. She'd made sure of that.

"The total will be seven-hundred-eighteen dollars and forty-three cents," the young man said.

Uncertainty rose as she looked from the portrait to the stack of hiking and camping paraphernalia. Even if by some miracle she succeeded on the trip, there was no way he'd let their firm handle his business. Not once he found out she was the account executive. She might as well give up now.

She'd have to tell Uncle Saul why. Would he keep her secret? No one in the family knew about her brief marriage to Hunter. Especially her mother. Heather never thought it would come out after all these years. Was there any way to get out of the trip and still keep the firm in the running?

No way that her flustered brain could come up with at the moment.

She looked at the salesclerk, patiently waiting. Fishing out her credit card, she handed it over, involuntarily looking once more at Hunter's face. A myriad of emotions chased through her. The dominant one was crushing sadness. She'd loved him so much. But circumstances and her own cruel words had ended their brief marriage before it had really begun.

She had treated him badly, running out as she had, contacting him through an attorney to end their marriage. She'd promised to love him forever, through sickness and health. And at the first crisis had run away, forsaking her young husband.

At the time she'd been sure it was for the best. Maybe

not for her, but for her mother, her family, and even for Hunter. Had he ever come to see it that way? She doubted it.

Heather spent the rest of the weekend reading the how-to camping books she had checked out from the library and hunting up shows on the Discovery channel dealing with the outdoors.

She also went on the Internet and read what she found about Trails West and its founders. It was as if she were reading the biography of a stranger. She recognized the university they'd both attended, but the rest was unknown information. So much had happened to Hunter after she'd left him, so much she had never been part of.

The possibility of running into Hunter at some future meeting if Jackson and Prince obtained the Trails West account was never far from her mind. She wished she could concentrate more on the hiking aspects the books described, but couldn't get Hunter out of her mind. What would he say if he learned she was in the running for their account in Seattle?

Frustrated with her own thoughts, Heather donned her jeans and new hiking boots and headed out for a walk. Maybe the fresh air would clear her head.

"Heather?" Her mother was in the living room, working on some quilting. She looked up as Heather came into the room. Frowning at her daughter's attire, she said, "Whatever are you dressed up for?"

"I told you about the camping trip Uncle Saul insists I take. I'm going for a walk. The salesclerk advised I break in the boots before the trip."

"How your uncle Saul can send you out into the wilderness like this is beyond me. Doesn't he know the dangers? You could be killed by a bear or wolf. Then where would I be? I'm calling him to tell him you cannot go."

"I need to go, Mom. Don't get involved." She didn't think the trip would be life-threatening. Trails West wanted to eliminate uninformed agencies, not kill them off.

"Don't get involved? How much more involved could I be when I'm being shunted over to that woman's house for a week? You know I don't like Susan," Amelia whined.

"You can stay here if you like," Heather said, moving to the door. She didn't need this added pressure. It was hard enough trying to focus on how she'd make it through the proposed weeding-out process, and how to avoid Hunter if she should make the short list. For once, couldn't her mother be supportive?

Amelia put her hand on her heart and caught her breath. "Heather, I can't be on my own. You know that."

Heather knew Susan thought her mother could. Since her mother rarely did anything around the house, Heather didn't believe that. Most people with disabilities coped, but her mother had a difficult time.

"I know, Mom. Susan and Saul will take good care of you. I'll be back in a bit."

She slipped out of the apartment and headed for the stairs. Normally she used the elevator to their fourth-floor apartment, but not today. She had to get used to more exercise, so might as well start here and now.

She hoped Susan and Saul would take good care of her mother, but Aunt Susan had long maintained millions of wheelchair-bound men and women lived perfectly well on their own, working, managing a home and often a family. Her aunt had told Heather more than once her mother was capable of managing on her own, but would rather have Heather at her beck and call instead.

Sometimes Heather believed that was true, then guilt would surface and once again, she stifled any inclinations for her own independence, grateful her mother had lived after the terrible crash that had killed her father.

An hour later Heather took the elevator back to the fourth floor. She was only up to so much exercise. The salesclerk had been right about needing to break in the hiking boots. She felt a blister rubbing on her left foot. She had time to take care of it before it got worse, but what if she'd started the trip with new boots? Time to pay strict attention to all the hints the clerk had given her. And all the material in the books she'd checked out.

The next two weeks passed quickly. Heather faithfully wore her camping attire every day—despite the raised eyebrows and comments at work. She spent every lunch hour walking up the hills of Seattle. She walked to and from work, and took the stairs every chance she got. She knew she wasn't in the best of shape, but at least had done what she could to prepare.

When home in the evening, she packed and repacked her backpack and practiced wearing it for an hour or two at a time. At first it was awkward but she grew used to it and by the end of the second week could easily walk up and down the stairs with it on.

Her mother argued with her every day, trying to talk her out of the foolishness, as she called it. But the closer the day came, the more determined Heather was to make a good showing. She owed it to her uncle, and to herself.

Hunter Braddock might not let Jackson and Prince have the account in the end, but it wouldn't be because it wasn't the most qualified firm in the running.

Finally the fateful Saturday arrived. She carefully re-packed her backpack according to the instructions given. She brought very few personal items, resigned to hand lotion as the only moisturizer she'd use, plus the sunscreen she'd brought. The hat she chose was the kind that could be scrunched up and then shaken out. Her clothes would end up wrinkled, but so would everyone else's she reasoned.

The only extras she brought were a digital camera and a journal and pencils. Might as well take advantage of the trip to capture images and ideas for future ads.

She was alone in the apartment as she finished packing. Her mother had gone to Saul's the night before, protesting every mile of the way.

Aunt Susan had been as gracious as could be, but everyone knew her feelings about Amelia's dependence on Heather. It could have been more awkward, but Heather dashed out before she had to listen to more of her mother's complaints. Let Saul deal with them. If he hadn't insisted she make the trip, he wouldn't have Amelia staying with them.

Hoisting the backpack, she slipped into the harness and adjusted it. She was as ready as she was going to be. Glancing around the apartment, she wished she could just cozy up with a good book and relax the weekend away.

Before long, however, she placed the pack in the trunk of her small car and headed toward the Cascades. The rendezvous point was a couple of hours from Seattle. She settled in to drive, butterflies dancing in her stomach. She hoped she could hold her own with the others participating in the hike.

As the miles sped by, Heather felt a curious sense of freedom. It had been years and years since she had much time away from her mother. Not that she had to be with her every moment, but overnight trips were almost impossible unless someone came to stay with Amelia. Heather didn't have a lot of friends. She had too little time to spend with them. Her mother's only interests were in quilting, so she didn't leave home often.

As she let her thoughts wander, Heather wondered how different her life would have been had that fateful car crash never happened. She'd lost her father at age nineteen and assumed responsibility for her mother when she should have still been carefree, studying at the university, planning her future. Building her marriage.

Of course, neither of her parents had known of her marriage. They had harped so much on her responsibility to get a good education, she was reluctant to tell them how involved she'd become with Hunter. When she tried to share her happiness with them at Christmas break, tried to tell them she'd met a man she thought was special, they'd really come done on her—reiterating that her goal should be graduation, nothing else. So she'd married in February without telling them, convinced once they saw her grades at the end of the year, they'd know she could handle marriage and college.

What heady days those had been. She'd been so much in love with Hunter. And he with her. They thought they had the entire world at their feet. She was going to get her degree in education and teach. He was already halfway through a business degree, planning on building an empire.

If Trails West was any indication, he was well on his way to achieving his goal.

She had never even finished her freshman year.

Sighing softly, Heather wondered what Hunter was like these days? Had he remarried? Did he have children?

The thought hurt. They hadn't talked about children during their brief period of married bliss. But she'd always expected to have a houseful. She was an only child and had so often envied her cousin Fletcher and his brothers and sisters. She loved it as a child when they'd spent holidays with the Owens family. There had been so much going on, laughter, heated discussions, and an abundance of love.

If she had one wish, it would be that the car crash never happened. But if she had two, it would be to change the way she had walked out of Hunter's life and ruthlessly ended something that had been so precious.

As she approached the Cascades, the topography changed. Hills rose and fell. Soaring pines and firs flanked the road. Signs of civilization grew farther and farther apart. Pristine streams crossed beneath arched bridges. It was lovely. Heather still wasn't sure about this trip, but she made up her mind to enjoy every aspect for as long as she lasted.

When the sign for Bear River Resort appeared, she

knew she was close. Nervousness built. Her entire future could be decided on a silly camping trip in the wilderness. How far-fetched was that?

The rustic lodge came into view when she rounded the corner. Following the instructions sent, she parked near the far left side. There were two men standing near a clearing, backpacks at their feet. Probably others going on the trip.

She took her backpack from the trunk and slung it over one shoulder. Walking over to the two men she smiled brightly. "Are you here for the Trails West camping trip?" she asked.

One man nodded, looking at her from head to toe. "You going?" he asked.

"That's right." Feigning more confidence than she felt, she put her backpack on the ground near the others.

"I'm Bill Evans, from Tierney and Ross Advertising," the second man said, stepping up eagerly holding out his hand. He shook hers firmly and smiled. "I wonder what other surprises I'll find. I expected this to be a male-only hike."

Heather smiled politely, introducing herself and her firm.

"John Murden," the other man said. "Statton Brothers." One of Seattle's leading agencies.

From the well-worn signs of his clothing and boots, he was very familiar with hiking wilderness trails, Heather thought.

"Interesting way to determine who gets the account, I think," Bill said.

"Inspired, I'd say," John said. "Weed those who write

hype from those who enjoy the real thing. I've been camping all my life. Trails West provides some of the best equipment in the business. No problem writing good ads when I believe in the product so strongly myself. I'm glad they're branching out into our part of the country."

Heather nodded, feeling totally out of place. Why had she thought she had a chance? Just looking at John made her want to turn around and head for home. He was obviously an experienced camper!

Another car turned into the parking lot. In only moments a third man joined their small group.

"Peter Howard," he said, striding in confidently. "With Howard, Mercell and Baker. I didn't expect so many taking part."

"The packet said there'd be five," Heather murmured. She introduced herself and listened while the others completed the ritual.

"I saw that, but still didn't expect everyone to show. This is taking valuable time away from the office. As a partner in our firm, I can afford it, but most account executives can't," he said, looking at Heather. "And I must say, little lady, you've got balls. Not too many women would want to pack into the wilderness for days on end with scruffy men. Can you stay the course or will we be requesting an emergency evacuation before the first day's out?" He laughed, but Heather wasn't amused.

"I plan to stay the course," she said firmly, hoping her pounding heart didn't give away her nervousness. She wished they could get started.

A black SUV turned into the lot, followed immediately by a dark red rental car. Both vehicles parked near Heather's car. The last two members of the group.

The man who climbed out of the rental car looked like a cowboy. He wore a Stetson and his jeans were worn at the knees. His boots were standard hiking issue, however.

He carried his backpack as if it weighed mere ounces.

But her attention was quickly drawn to the man getting out of the SUV. For a moment time stood still. Then her heart rate kicked into double-time. Heat rose in her face. Her worst nightmare. She couldn't believe it.

Hunter Braddock slammed the door, hefted a backpack in one hand and a bulging duffel bag in another and headed for the clearing.

CHAPTER TWO

HUNTER quickly scanned the group waiting in the clearing, noting the backpacks piled together. He hoped Alan knew what he was doing trying for a new angle to get the best ad agency on board. It didn't necessarily mean because a man could hike into the back country that he was a media expert.

Or woman, he amended when he noted one of the people was female. Hell of a note, he thought. He was substituting for Alan at the last minute, and had only brought three tents. Logistics would prove difficult.

As he drew closer, he almost stopped dead. *The woman was Heather.*

He caught his breath for a second, not believing what he saw. The last time he'd seen Heather, she'd run from their apartment saying she never wanted to see him again.

What was she doing here?

"Hunter Braddock? Bill Evans, let me help you with that." One of the men from the group came to take the duffel. Hunter looked at him, tearing his gaze away from Heather.

"Thanks. Evans from Tierney and Ross?" Hunter

had jotted down the companies represented on the trek, with last names of the account representatives. He had never connected H. Jackson—with Jackson and Prince—to Heather.

For a moment the fact she'd taken back her last name after their divorced rankled. What had he expected? They'd only been married a few days beyond three months a long time ago. Water long over the dam.

He was here on business. Presumably she had made a good enough showing to be in the running. Alan didn't know their history, he would have chosen based on merit of the work submitted. Could he do so as well?

"Peter Howard, Hunter. Didn't expect the big man himself to be with us. Glad you could make it." Peter stepped forward and offered his hand.

Hunter nodded, dropping his pack with the others. He shook Peter's hand. Then Bill Evans's and Jess Townsend's, the cowboy. Finally he turned to Heather.

Her eyes were wide, watching him warily. The dark brown color at such odds with her light hair still had the ability to fascinate him. She was slim and trim and looked like a polished doll. Clothes were new, nails were fake and her hairstyle wouldn't last a day. She'd be gone before nightfall. He couldn't believe she'd even made a showing.

"Heather," he said. There was no need to offer his hand. He didn't want to touch that soft skin again. He knew how it felt. For a moment, his fingertips almost tingled in remembered response to the satiny texture.

"Hunter," she said.

He saw the effort she made to keep her expression

impassive. Did she expect anything special from him? If so, she was doomed to disappointment. He had nothing for her. Just as she had nothing for him. What they'd had burned out long ago.

Turning his back on her he glanced at the others.

"Alan Osborne was supposed to lead the trek, but he broke his ankle two days ago in a motocross accident. I've just gotten in from Denver, so we'll cut the first day short since I'm beat. I assume everyone brought all the things listed. I brought the tents. We'll take turns carrying them. They're lightweight, two-men tents." He scanned the sky with a practiced eye. "The forecast is for clear skies for the next few days with a possibility of rain later in the week, so let's hope the weather holds."

Peter laughed. "If the tents only hold two, I'll volunteer to share with Heather," he said, leering over at her.

Hunter drew in his breath. He hadn't seen the woman in ten years. She no longer meant anything to him. But the other man had just rubbed him the wrong way.

"Heather shares with me," he said flatly.

"You're holding the winning hand, you get to call the shots," Peter said. "Maybe we should rotate every night. That would be fair."

"I don't need a tent. I can sleep out under the stars," Heather said quickly.

Hunter ignored the comment. "If we're ready to go, I suggest we get started. Everyone has everything they need? Anyone need a pit stop before we head out?"

"Yes."

He turned. Heather was already heading toward the

lodge. He watched her walk away, remembering the last time she'd walked away. He'd thought the world had come to an end. Anger flared briefly. And a bittersweet acceptance that life had not played out as he'd once thought it would.

"I'll go, too," Jess said, ambling behind Heather.

The others began talking to Hunter about the trail ahead, the first campsite and what he hoped to accomplish by the trip. Hunter turned away from Heather and focused on the men in front of him.

"I'm hoping to get to know you better, hear what your vision is for the future of Trails West promotion and give you what you need to give us the best service possible," he said. "Alan's idea was if our account executive was knowledgeable in one area of our products, it would weigh in heavily in the media coverage. Of course, we'd like the AE's to be knowledgeable in all areas, to some extent, at least."

"You'd get that from Howard, Mercell and Baker," Peter said confidently. "Hiking, skiing, football, soccer, whatever, someone in our firm is an expert."

Hunter shrugged. "Early days yet, Peter. We'll have to see, won't we."

Heather used the facilities, reluctant to leave the safety of the ladies' room. She washed her hands, splashing water on her face. Staring at her reflection, she swallowed hard. She hadn't been sure she could manage before, now she knew she'd never last a week with Hunter.

Share a tent with him? Not likely. What had he been thinking?

Not that she wanted to sleep next to Peter Howard, either.

She didn't need a tent. She would just find a flat place and sleep outside. Wasn't that the whole point of the trip—get close to nature using Trails West products? The weather was supposed to be fine. Maybe if it rained, she'd have to share, but not unless dire circumstances so dictated.

"Tell them you didn't know it would be an all-man expedition. That you've changed your mind," she said slowly to herself, grappling to find a last minute get-out clause.

And with that, she'd lose all chance of getting the account for Jackson and Prince, which her uncle insisted they needed. Always the dutiful family member, she took a deep breath determined to give it her best shot. She felt the weight of responsibility press down. Why was she the one always needed to keep things going? Not for the first time she wished she had an older brother on whom the duties of the family could fall.

She headed back to the group. No matter what, she wasn't quitting. Jackson and Prince depended upon her, just as her mother did.

Hunter seemed surprised to see her return. Had he thought she'd bow out just because he showed up? She reached for her pack. A lot of years had gone by since she'd walked out of their marriage. Maybe it was time to show Hunter what she was made of now. She hoped it would be enough to erase the impressions of the past, and let him know she could be depended upon—in business at least.

Forget the past, the next week was what counted.

* * *

Hunter gave Jess and John a tent each, tying one onto his own backpack. Compact, they took up little room and weighed only a few pounds. Shrugging into his pack, he watched as the others donned theirs. Heather wasn't as at ease putting hers on as the others were. But Hunter resisted any instinct to help. Let her manage herself, he wasn't doing anyone on the trip any special favors.

In less than ten minutes, everyone was ready to go.

He led off. Heather watched as Peter immediately joined him, talking about the plans his firm had for media explosions.

"Sounds dangerous," Jess murmured, walking beside her while watching Peter monopolize Hunter.

"Do you think he's going to talk shop nonstop?" she asked.

He shrugged. "It's what we're here for, to toot our own horn and make Hunter realize our firm is best."

She looked at him surprised at the idea. "Really? I thought it was to test out the product and become familiar with it."

The others were strung out along the beginning of the trail. Jess nodded and Heather followed John and Bill, with him beside her.

"I already know about the products. My firm is based in Denver and we have the Denver account. We didn't bid for the California sites and my boss has been on my case ever since. We want the Pacific Northwest stores if we can get them. We've been the agency in Denver since they started. We know their products."

"They're good," she said. "And I like the way their clerks are specialists in different fields so they can really help customers." She had her own experience to go by, and was grateful the salesclerk had been so knowledgeable.

"That's a major plus of each store. The starter gear, for whatever sport, also has great instructions."

So it wasn't enough to survive the trip, pretend she was enjoying herself and get experience with the product. Heather also was supposed to convince Hunter her agency was his best choice.

She almost laughed at the irony. Fletcher should have come. Or anyone else. Her presence would doom their chance.

The trail was packed earth dusted with pine and fir needles, with only a gradual incline. Before long, Jess dropped behind her and fell quiet. She could hear Peter talking nonstop, not the words, just the rise and fall of his voice. Was Hunter intrigued, or annoyed?

Ignoring the others, Heather looked around. It was beautiful in the forest. The trees soared high overhead, the trunks straight and dark. The trail was covered with old needles, giving it a springing feel as they walked quietly along. Occasionally she heard a rustling nearby, but she never saw the animal causing the noise.

The air was fresh and clean and as she fell into the rhythm of the hike, she gradually let the tension fade. She'd do her best, that's all she could do. When her uncle expressed regret they didn't get the account, she'd at least know she'd done all she could have done. The deck was stacked against them from the get-go.

Hunter hoped to hell there was a clearing soon. When they reached one, he planned to call a rest and find a way to switch the order of the line. If he had to listen to Peter Howard all day every day of the hike, he'd go stark-raving bonkers. The man was a braggart and boasted of impossible feats. He might be a great copywriter, but his personality left much to be desired.

He knew Jess from Denver. At least the two of them could discuss the chances of the Broncos going to the Super Bowl or what the skiing might be like in the coming winter.

He knew he'd have to have a one-on-one time with each of the participants. He was not looking forward to spending any time alone with Heather.

Why had he made that asinine comment about her sharing his tent? Let her fend for herself. If she liked men like Peter, more power to her. Hunter was no longer her protector, no longer anything to her. She'd made that perfectly clear when she'd chosen her family over him so many years ago.

He tried to tune Peter out as he reviewed the reason for the trek. Alan's idea didn't seem so brilliant under the circumstances. What was wrong with just picking the ad strategy that appealed and forget about the actual experience of the account executive? Experienced hikers didn't necessarily make the best ad copywriters.

But at the back of his mind the entire time was the knowledge Heather Jackson was walking twenty feet behind him. Was that the real reason he didn't like the idea of the trip?

He refused to let his mind drift back to the halcyon days of their brief marriage. He'd thought they'd be together forever. Yet the first crisis had split them apart.

When push came to shove, she chose her family over him. Did she ever regret walking out on him?

Too bad if she did. She'd caused their split. She could just live with the consequences. As she obviously had been doing. Without looking behind him, he could picture her. She looked slim and sleek. The fashionable hairstyle and fake nails proved her success in one sense, as did her being on the hike. Quite a change from his carefree young wife who had so wanted to teach.

After a sharp bend upward, he found a clearing. He stopped and unbuckled his pack.

"We stopping?" Peter asked, looking around. "I'm still raring to go. Of course if you need to give the others some downtime, I'm all for it. We want them to at least finish the first day, right?"

Hunter ignored him. There was no we in this equation. And at the rate Peter was going, Hunter would blacklist his firm forever just to make sure he didn't have to listen to the man talk endlessly.

One by one the others joined them.

"I'm calling a ten-minute rest," he said, avoiding Heather's eyes. "Then we'll rotate. That gives everyone time to talk to me. I'm hoping by tomorrow your presentations will have been made and we can enjoy the backpacking experience without jockeying for position. Any questions?"

John Murden nodded. "How involved do you want? I've been hiking before, and already use a lot of your products. Alan obviously liked what he saw of our presentation, or I wouldn't have made the short list. What more are you looking for?"

"Not much. I want a chance to get to know each of you, to see how we connect on a personal level." He almost cringed at his choice of words. He already knew how he had connected with Heather on a personal level. A quick glance at her and he saw she was frowning. It was a slip of words, he wanted to tell her, but kept his remarks impersonal and to the group.

"Have you seen the ads?" Jess asked.

"I brought them with me. They're in the car," Hunter said. "I skimmed them on the flight here, so you can fill me in on long-term plans and other aspects you've come up with. As I said, this is really Alan's baby, I'm just standing in."

"As president, however, what you say goes, right?" Peter asked.

Hunter nodded. He glanced at Heather again, but she was staring across the clearing, avoiding his eyes as he had avoided hers.

Jess sat down on the ground and leaned against his backpack. "Might as well take advantage of the rest time," he said. Settling his cowboy hat across his face, he seemed to drop off to sleep immediately.

Heather took off her pack, glad for the relief. She'd practiced wearing it over the last two weeks, but the couple of hours on the trail were already taking their toll. Her shoulders ached. She reached into the outer flap of the pack and drew out her camera. They had been pretty much hemmed in by trees, but she hoped they'd find some areas where the forest opened up and she could get a sweeping view. In the meantime, she'd snap some photos of the group. Jess sleeping was a perfect study.

John and Bill leaned against some nearby trees talking quietly, backpacks at their feet. Peter was still talking to Hunter. She quickly turned away. She was not taking any photographs of Hunter Braddock.

Though she longed to. Something to take home. To look at over the years ahead. How maudlin. She'd chosen her path a long time ago. No sense having regrets.

But they throbbed none the less. She wished so much over the last ten years that things had been different. That money had not been the pressing issue immediately after the car crash, and that the care her mother had initially needed hadn't taken every bit of energy she possessed.

And the nights, how long had it been before she had been able to fall asleep without crying for Hunter? Years, she remembered.

She rotated her shoulders, hoping she was up to the trek. Glancing at her watch she saw it was only two. Hours yet until they made camp. She gazed at the forest, feeling lonely. Everyone else had someone to talk to, except Jess who was sleeping.

In only moments Hunter called them to get going again.

This leg Peter rotated to the rear, Jess in front of him, with Heather one person closer to Hunter. Peter didn't let his being ousted at the front slow his conversation. He told Jess how his firm was expanding, how successful it was in the Seattle area, and how he expected it to explode with growth when acquiring firms such as Trails West.

Jess listened for a while then told him to shut up, he wanted to enjoy nature, not Peter's bragging.

Heather smiled. She glanced over her shoulder and gave him a secret thumbs-up. He tipped his hat to her.

The silence was peaceful. She began to understand why people were drawn to hiking and camping. It afforded them a chance to draw close to nature and experience things forgotten in the hustle of a busy city.

For a brief period of time she didn't have to worry about her mother, fret about making ends meet, or dream dreams that had long ago been forfeited.

She was surprised to find she was enjoying herself!

Three hours later Heather was ready to drop. She purposefully kept putting one foot in front of the other, but she had lost feeling in both legs ages ago. Her shoulders burned with the heavy weight of the backpack. Her head pounded with each jarring step she took. Each minute she thought she'd have to sink on the trail and let the others go on without her. But each time the thought came, she pushed it away and kept walking. She would not give up the first day!

They crossed a small stream, balancing on wide stepping stones. She thought once she was going to fall in, but easily made the other side still dry and on her feet.

"We'll make camp here tonight," Hunter said, slipping out of his backpack.

For a moment the words didn't penetrate. When they did she was almost euphoric. They were stopping. Hallelujah!

She unbuckled her waist strap and slipped the heavy pack from her shoulders. The relief was so sharp she almost cried out.

Glancing around, she took note of the wide expanse. Almost a meadow, there were only a few trees nearby.

The stream gurgled merrily over the rocks. It would be a soothing melody to sleep to.

"John and Bill, why don't you start the fire for dinner. Heather and Peter can gather wood. Jess, you get the water and help me scout out where to put the tents," Hunter directed. No one challenged his right to assign tasks.

Glad she wasn't paired up with Hunter, Heather looked around. The meadow was grassy, no sticks or twigs visible. Peter jerked his head. "Come with me, little lady. We'll find so much wood, we'll leave a pile for the next party to come this way."

Resigned to having to deal with Peter, she followed. Fortunately he acted as if he didn't expect her to have a single thought in her head. He pointed out deadfall, told her to gather as much as she could carry, and not to worry that she couldn't pull in as much as he would. No one expected her to.

Right then and there Heather vowed she would outlast Peter. No matter what, she would not see him get the account through her forfeit.

She gathered wood and headed back to the clearing. There was enough conversation from the others to guide her back. Three times she brought as much wood as she could carry, dumping it where John had indicated.

Peter worked hard, she had to give him that. But his constant talking was driving her crazy. And it wasn't work for its own sake, but for bragging rights. She wished she could shut him up as effectively as Jess had earlier.

John and Bill made quick work of a fire and Heather relished the warmth each time she drew close. The afternoon was fast waning and with the setting of the sun, the temperatures were plummeting as well. She'd put on her jacket as soon as she brought in one more armful.

"That'll do it," John said when she dumped her last load. "We'll have a fire all night long with the wood you two gathered."

She nodded and went to her pack, quickly pulling out the warm jacket she'd put on top.

"You okay?" Jess asked as he passed carrying one of the small tents.

"Fine."

He stopped, hesitated a moment. "I know it's none of my business, but you might wish to reconsider sleeping outside of a tent. The dew settles before dawn which gets the sleeping bags wet and you'll be colder than you ever thought you'd be. The tent will insulate us from the dew and the body heat from the occupants goes a long way to making it a more comfortable night."

"Can I share with you?" she asked suddenly. It wasn't so much she wanted to sleep alone under the stars, just not share a tight space with Hunter.

He glanced at Hunter, some distance away, effectively setting up one tent.

"Don't see why not. I'm not looking for the same thing Peter would be."

She grinned. "Thank God for that. All I want to do is crawl into my sleeping bag and sleep until dawn."

"First day's hard. Second's harder, then we get into the groove."

"I'll remember that."

"Jess, you helping, or talking?" Hunter called.

Heather could see his scowl from where she stood.

"Just giving me some advice," she called. "Thanks, Jess," she said, and turned to the fire. "What needs to be done next?" she asked as she approached.

Heather tried to stay out of Hunter's line of sight for the rest of the evening. She fetched her cooking gear, one of the meal packets and followed the instructions to make her dinner. The noodles and sauce were delicious. She ate every bite, washing it down with stream water that had been boiled to sanitize.

The men fell into friendly conversation sharing past experiences in camping adventure. John Murden seemed to have the most stories. Heather knew he liked to camp, and was very good at organizing and getting things done with minimum fuss. She laughed at some of his anecdotes while she ate.

By the time full darkness came, she was finished, had cleaned her utensils and was ready to crawl into her sleeping bag.

She had to make use of the bounty of nature and snapped off her flashlight when she was far enough away from the camp. She didn't want to take any chances with Peeping Toms.

Fortunately the fire glow and soft conversation was as good as a map for finding her way back to the camp.

Jess had set up a tent some distance from the fire. She grabbed her pack and headed there as Hunter rose from his place near the fire and approached.

"Where are you going?" he asked, looking at her pack.

"To bed. We'll be up by dawn, right?" She hoped she didn't sound as tired as she felt. If she didn't get horizontal soon, she'd fall flat on her face.

"Our tent is that way." He pointed to the one he'd set up near the perimeter.

Our tent? It had a warm sound to it, but Heather wasn't moved.

"Thanks, but Jess said I could bunk in with him." She stepped around him and started for the tent only to have him grab her arm and spin her around.

"You are not sleeping with Jess Townsend," he said.

She shook her arm free. "Whom I sleep with is none of your concern."

"Are you two involved?" he asked ominously.

"I met him today. As I did the others. But he seems the less threatening of all of you."

"Don't let that good ole boy facade fool you. Jess is as much a man as anyone."

She blinked. "What are you talking about?"

"The only man here immune to your charms is me. Stick with who you know," Hunter said.

"You act as if I'm some femme fatale. I'm going to get into my sleeping bag and go to sleep. That's it."

"You stay warmer if you get out of your clothes," he said. "Are you planning to disrobe with Jess in the tent?"

She frowned. She remembered the salesclerk mentioning something about taking off her jeans to stay more comfortable during the night. She hadn't paid that much attention at the time. Surely she'd stay warmer with more clothes on.

"I'm not planning to disrobe at all," she snapped.

"Be a cold, uncomfortable night if you don't."

"I'll make do."

He looked as if he planned to say something else, but changed his mind and clamped his mouth shut.

"So be it. Good night." He turned back to the fire.

Heather headed for the tent, feeling she'd won that round. But doubts filled her. Was Jess expecting more than a tent mate? He'd not flirted with her at all. Seemed to ignore her most of the time. Ignore everyone, if she thought about it.

She glanced at the fire. Hunter had returned and hunkered down near the flames. Probably getting warm. It was decidedly cooler away from the heat.

She thrust her backpack into the small tent and crawled in behind it. In less than five minutes she was zipped up in her sleeping bag, snuggled down hoping it would warm up soon. The inflatable mattress she'd blown up eased her back. In only moments, she relaxed enough to fall asleep.

Heather awoke to the sound of birds chattering in the trees. She smiled at the sound. She rarely noticed birds chirping at home, too few trees, too much traffic. The sound of the creek splashing over the rocks provided the soothing background she'd remembered from yesterday. It was a perfect site for camping. She hoped all their campgrounds would be as peaceful and delightful.

Reluctant to leave the warmth, Heather snuggled into the sleeping bag. It was cold outside, the tip of her nose told her that. She strained her ears, but heard no one stirring. Turning in her bag, she eyed the man sleeping beside her, covered completely with only a few wisps of dark hair showing. She wondered if she could get dressed and out of the tent without waking him. She reached over her head for her jeans and pulled them in the sleeping bag, squirming around until she pulled them on. They were cold, but warmed quickly enough in the confining bag.

Slowly she zipped down the side of the bag, hoping the rasp wouldn't waken Jess.

She glanced over to make sure he was still sleeping—stunned to see Hunter's steely-gray eyes gazing back at her.

CHAPTER THREE

"WHAT are you doing here?" she snapped, conscious of the others nearby.

"Being awakened before I wanted, obviously," Hunter said. He sat up, the sleeping bag dropping from his shoulders.

From his tanned and *bare* shoulders, Heather noted.

She looked away before the sight of his muscular physique awakened memories of other mornings when they awoke together. Had he worn nothing to bed? The thought was provocative. She wanted to know, yet if true, knew the knowledge would prove nothing but dangerous to her equilibrium.

"I'm going to use a tree," she said, pushing her sleeping bag out of her way and putting on one shoe. She couldn't escape the tent fast enough. "What happened to Jess?"

"We agreed to switch tents," Hunter said easily, watching her.

Her fingers shaking, Heather fumbled with the laces. She was aware of Hunter's nearness. His attention. His bare shoulders!

"Start the fire when you're done," he said.

She nodded, hoping she could do that simple task. She put on her other shoe and reached into her backpack for tissue. She felt as if she were moving through cold molasses. Time seemed to stand still. She wanted out. Fumbling for the matches, she located the waterproof tin and clutched it gratefully. She donned her jacket and without saying another word, crawled from the tent, extremely conscious of Hunter's gaze on her every second.

"I hope he got an eyeful," she muttered as she headed into the brush. "And wished for things to be different!"

A few minutes later she washed her hands and splashed frigid water on her face. The cool mountain air felt even colder as the water dried. She prayed she could get a fire going, she was freezing.

It took six attempts, but she finally succeeded. Slowly she fed the growing flames with some of the wood gathered last night. Feeling justifiably proud, she looked up when Hunter exited their tent. He glanced around the clearing and frowned, then headed for the fire.

Heather held her ground. If she had any hope of getting the account, she had to demonstrate she could work with Hunter.

"Should I get water to start for coffee?" she asked, trying to treat him as she would Jess or John.

"I'll get it." He snagged a small bucket and went to the creek.

He sat across from her when he returned, balancing the bucket on the flames.

"I expected the others to be up. If they don't get up on their own soon, I'll waken them."

She nodded.

Silence reigned.

Heather wasn't sure what to say. She glanced at him, startled to find he was staring at her.

"How did you get into advertising?" he asked. "I thought you were going to become a teacher."

"I never made it back to college," she said. "My mother was several years recovering. My uncle owns the agency. He gave me my start. But I'm still there because I'm good." She didn't want him to think their agency wasn't up to the standards of Trails West.

"Mmm," was the only reply.

He looked terrific in the early morning. He had a shadow on his jaw, needing a shave. His hair was slightly tousled, giving rise to an urge to run her fingers through it. She swallowed and looked away, trying to damp down the longings that filled her.

She stared at the water in the pot, wishing she could find the words to ease the tension between them. She'd been the one to walk out. She owed him an apology at the very least.

"Hunter, I—"

"Hey, I thought I'd be first up, should have known I couldn't beat you out, Hunter," Peter said crossing the meadow. "Fine day." He rubbed his hands together, ignoring Heather. "Can't wait to get started. That's the great thing about working with accounts like yours, we can combine business with pleasure."

Her eyes met Hunter's for a moment. He had to know she'd been going to say something important before Peter intruded. But he looked away without acknowledgment.

"Today's trek will take us up to a higher elevation, with some steep climbs. But the views are supposed to be spectacular," Hunter said. "The sooner everyone is up and eats, the sooner we can get started."

Heather faded into the background as the others joined in. She knew she should make more of an effort to participate, but in light of their past, she didn't think there was much point. The men seemed to have no trouble talking easily among themselves. She felt very left out.

There was time enough for her to jot some notes in her journal before they broke camp and started. She wanted to capture her impressions of the trip, and note aspects she could punch up in ad copy. If not for the Trails West account, maybe for another store at some time. The brook was one feature of this campsite she really enjoyed. What she'd learned about cooking on the open fire would make good copy.

She knew it might be pointless to continue, but on the off chance they had a shot at the account, she wanted to bring it her best efforts.

She paused in her writing a little later and looked up, searching in her mind for the right word. Her eyes connected with Hunter's. She felt as if he'd touched her. Longings rose again. She couldn't turn back the clock. Couldn't change life. But could they reach a state of neutrality? Would he even want to try?

John joined Hunter this morning when they began the hike. Heather hung back. Peter and Bill had had turns with Hunter, now it was John's turn. Would hers come this afternoon? Did she have to talk business, or dare she try to explain what had happened so long ago? Would she find him more sympathetic, or still as difficult to deal with? She wasn't sure she wanted to find out. But she felt honor-bound to offer an apology.

As Hunter had predicted, the trail grew more difficult. It wound around the mountain, rising every step. Heather had to pull herself up a couple of times, holding on to rocks or trees because it was so steep. Hunter and John had no difficulties, she noted. She hoped he wasn't watching her, judging her abilities, but every time she looked ahead, she seemed to see Hunter's disapproving gaze.

At one particular steep juncture, Hunter halted and waited until everyone caught up. Studying the bank, he assessed the twenty-foot face for the easiest route.

"Alan mapped out the hike," he said. "I think this is one of the hardest parts of the entire trail. Once we have this behind us, it'll be back to a fairly easy climb." Glancing around the group, he added, "I'm open for any suggestions."

Heather wondered if it were a test. She looked at the wall of dirt and rock ahead of them. It looked perpendicular at first glance, but as she studied it, she could see that while it was very steep, there were undulations in the surface and if they traversed the face, it wouldn't be impossible.

"Seems to be a faint trail." John pointed after scanning the surface.

"Probably an animal trail. And where a deer can go, so can we," Peter said. "Want me to go up first?"

Hunter shook his head. "I'll go. Once on the top, I'll

lower a rope and draw the packs up that way. No sense trying the ascent wearing them. It's too bad the trail doesn't
go straight up, we could use a rope as a guide, then."

In only a few moments he was at the top of the cliff,
making the climb look easy. He tossed down a rope for
his backpack. One by one, they tied on their packs and
Hunter pulled them to the top. When all the gear was
with him, he motioned for them to begin.

"I'll go next," Peter said, swaggering to the base. He
followed Hunter's path, slipping twice, but grabbing on
to a protruding rock each time to stop his fall.

Bill went next. He also slipped in almost the same
locations as Peter.

"Watch it," he called down when he reached the top.
"The rock is real loose there and slippery as shale."

"Too bad they can't toss the rope down for us," John
said. But as Hunter had already mentioned, the path up
was too erratic for a rope dropped straight down.

"See you at the top," Jess said, heading for the
faint path.

Heather grew more and more nervous watching each
hiker take the trail. She had to go next if she didn't want
to be last. But it looked so intimidating. And if experienced hikers had trouble, how would she manage?

Slowly Jess moved up the face. When he reached the
first slippery spot, he quickly moved over it. He wasn't
as fortunate at the next one, spinning around and sliding
until he lost his balance completely and fell over the side
bouncing down to the flat space near Heather and John.

"Oh my God," she said, dashing over. Jess rolled
over and sat up, clutching his left leg.

"Damn, that hurts," he said through gritted teeth.

"Stay calm," Heather said. She and John reached him at almost the same time.

"Leg broken?" John asked.

"Not my leg, my ankle could be. Don't know if it's broken or just sprained, but it hurts like a son of a gun," Jess said. He was pale with shock, and continued to hold his ankle.

Heather knelt beside him, gently feeling his ankle through the hiking boot. "Either way, you're going to swell up soon. I think we should get the boot off as quickly as possible, and get something cold on the ankle. Too bad we aren't still by that stream, it was cold as ice."

Hunter joined them a moment later. Heather looked at him in surprise. She hadn't heard him descend.

"How are you?" he asked Jess.

"I'll make it."

Heather gingerly felt the swelling skin. She rotated his foot gently. "I'm not a doctor, but I do know first aid and I don't think he's broken anything. But he needs X-rays to confirm that. My first-aid kit is in my backpack."

"I brought mine," Hunter said, handing her the compact plastic box.

With John and Hunter watching, she soon had the ankle taped.

"We need something cold to keep the swelling down," she said.

"I'll get one of the men on top to search out a stream. Any water around here will be cold enough," Hunter said.

"Thanks," Jess said. He lay back against a tree, still pale. "Damn stupid thing to do. I got cocky, after making it through that first stretch." He looked at Heather. "You be careful when you go up that trail, it's like walking on marbles."

She nodded, wondering if she'd get the chance to try. Surely they'd cancel the trip at this point.

"This certainly puts paid to my completing the course," Jess said to Hunter.

"We'll call Search and Rescue and see if they can come in to get you to a hospital. We'll sort things out later," Hunter said. "John, go tell the others the plan. See if Peter or Bill can find a stream and bring us back some cold water. In the meantime…" He fished in his pocket and brought out a cell phone. Clicking it on, he checked for a signal.

"Don't have any signal here, I'll have to hike out until I get one. Heather, you'll stay with Jess. Do what you can to make him comfortable."

It was almost four o'clock by the time a Search and Rescue team arrived to take charge. Peter and Bill had found some water and brought a canteen full, joining the rest on the lower level with Jess. The men had talked idly while they'd waited. Heather had listened staying near Jess until the Search and Rescue team arrived.

Without delay, Jess was transported out by stretcher to a place where the S&R helicopter had landed. The rest of them trailed them until they saw Jess was taken care of.

Just before he was carried off, he signaled Heather to come closer.

She leaned over him.

"Sorry we didn't get to share a tent," he said. "Since

our company won't get the account, I hope yours does. We might do some ad campaigns together."

She smiled at him and patted his shoulder. "I'll look forward to it. Take care of yourself."

Hunter watched as Jess said something private to Heather which brought a smile to her lips. He looked away, angry he couldn't seem to keep her from dominating his thoughts. If Jess were staying, he'd tell the man not to count on Heather. She promised forever and only gave three months.

Or maybe it was just with him. Though he didn't believe she remarried, there was no ring on her finger, or any indication she'd worn one. He still had the one he'd bought for her. The one they'd pledged their love with. The one she'd thrown at him before leaving that last day.

More fool him for keeping it. He'd get rid of it when he returned home. Why had he held on to it for all these years? He knew she was never coming back.

Mindful of accidents which Jess proved could easily happen, Hunter took care to make sure everyone reviewed the basics before challenging the cliff again. Heather carefully followed his instructions, her heart catching in her throat when her foot slipped near where Jess had fallen. But she made it to the top without mishap.

They made camp in a small clearing not too far from the cliff. It was too late to make the originally planned site.

There was no water except what they each carried in their canteens. Making a sparse meal, Hunter gave Heather the tent he'd taken from Jess.

"You get a place to yourself tonight," he said.

"Thanks." She looked at it, and at him, smiling brightly. She didn't want him to know she hadn't a clue how to set it up.

He suspected, however. Crossing his arms over his chest he looked as if he wasn't moving for a millennium. "Did you take the time to learn how to put it up before coming on this trip?"

"Actually I was hoping the instructions were included so I could see if they were written for a novice. That would make great ad copy, instructions so clear even a first time camper can manage."

His eyes narrowed. "Good recovery," he said, turning away.

A few moments later he returned with a sheet of paper in hand. "Directions."

Heather set out to show Hunter she could manage. She followed the directions to the letter and in a short time had the tent erected. Feeling triumphant, she turned and smiled. "My compliments to your documentation writers, these instructions are clear and easy to follow."

"You've changed, Heather," he said.

Immediately she went on the defensive. Now. She had to apologize now.

"I'm sorry for the way I left. I was distraught. I shouldn't have said all the things I did. But I felt so guilty."

"Water over the dam, a long time ago. Is your mother doing okay?"

"She's confined to a wheelchair and needs a lot of care, but she's doing all right given her limitations."

She waited, hoping he'd ask if she were doing okay, but he didn't. He merely nodded and returned to the fire.

Thanks to the delay caused by Jess's accident, the afternoon's hike had been quite short. Heather wasn't nearly as tired as she had been the night before. Still, she decided to make an early night and brought her things to the tent and crawled in. No one had explained why Hunter had been the man to share her tent, and now it didn't matter. She had one to herself.

She used her small flashlight to write in her journal, then flicked it off to settle in her sleeping bag.

It was more difficult to fall asleep tonight than last night. She kept seeing Hunter, a mixture of the strong man leading the hike and the younger man so determined to make something of himself.

He'd come from a family who didn't have much. When the factory where his father worked had been closed, his parents had been hard put to make ends meet. His mother had left shortly after that. He'd seen how demoralizing the loss of work and results had been for his father, and had told Heather over and over he would never let that happen to him.

By sheer determination and monumental effort, he worked to put himself through college. Scholarships had been in short supply, and he had not considered student loans, not wishing to start life with such a handicap. By working, pulling in great grades, he was walking a fine line.

She'd admired him so much back then.

Yet, hadn't history almost replayed itself? Hunter's wife had left as well. She hadn't thought about the correlation before. She wouldn't blame him if he never trusted a woman again.

Was he involved with someone? She was fascinated by him today. He easily took charge, and the other men naturally looked to him for leadership. He'd handled the crisis with Jess calmly and efficiently, and never made the other man feel stupid or clumsy for having fallen.

When she heard him speaking with the others, she strained to listen. His voice was deep and sexy.

She blinked and frowned. No, she was not going there. She had lived without him for ten years and didn't need old fantasies starting up again.

Heather had missed him so much when she first returned home. Had she seen anyway clear to making their life as he'd hoped to have it, she would have fought everyone and everything to return.

But she couldn't saddle him with an invalid mother-in-law and a wife whose loyalties were so divided. There had been no hope of a speedy recovery, or an easy way and she hadn't wished to tie him down.

Look how he had soared. Trails West was a strong concern, growing and expanding and fitting into communities in a way that had to bring a lot of satisfaction to its founders. She wished she'd been a part of it from the beginning.

But life was as it was. Her mother needed her, in spite of her aunt Susan's contention that Amelia milked her limitations for all they were worth. Heather wondered if her mother would ever want her to marry, to build a family apart from her. She claimed she needed too much attention herself to ever release Heather. Yet Aunt Susan's words were starting to sink in. Had she put herself at her mother's beck and call needlessly as the years had moved on? There was no doubt she'd been essential at the beginning, but now?

With a sad sigh, she turned over and tried to concentrate on going to sleep, and not dream about life with Hunter Braddock, either past or future.

Because of fitful sleep, Heather woke late the next morning. She heard the others at the campfire, banging utensils against the pans, talking, soft male laughter. Almost groaning, she quickly dressed. Her shoulders felt stiff, and her back ached. She held to the comment Jess had made that this day would be easier. She hoped so.

Would there be any word about him, or were they out of cell phone range again?

The only good thing to come of yesterday's mishap was she didn't have her one-on-one with Hunter. Today, however, with Jess gone, she was the only one of the group who had not yet spent time at the front of the line discussing ad strategies with the head of Trails West.

She would make sure she got her time with him. She may not get the account, but it wouldn't be for lack of trying. And she hoped Hunter had retained his sense of fairness to give her a hearing.

When they started out, Peter joined Hunter in the lead. Had it been anyone else, Heather might have let it go, postponing her confrontation with her former husband. But Peter annoyed her.

"I believe it's my turn to talk to Hunter," she said, joining them. The trail was narrow, necessitating single file travel. But where it widened, she was going to be the one with Hunter, not Peter the Braggart.

"I thought you might want to talk to him when we took a break," Peter said.

"I have more to say than ten minutes' worth," she bluffed. She refused to look at Hunter, knowing instinctively he would not take her part. But she vowed she would make a pitch for her firm, even if he asked to have another account executive be in charge of the account.

Peter backed down with poor grace. "Go for it little lady. Need to keep everyone happy."

She smiled at him. "Absolutely!" She wanted to knock his head off, but contented herself with winning that round.

That is until she saw Hunter. His expression was hard to read. Was he angry?

Or amused? She almost suspected the latter, but he turned and strode off without a word. Hurrying to catch up, she couldn't talk for watching where she was going and trying to keep pace.

Around a bend, Hunter stopped abruptly and she caromed into him. His hands gripped her arms, steadying her.

She looked up into his eyes. They were dark grey. Around each eye fine lines radiated outward, like he laughed a lot. Did he, when he wasn't around her, that was? His skin was smooth and tanned, his jaw firm, jutting just a little. She knew he was stubborn, she'd had plenty of evidence of that over the brief time she'd known him before. His jaw confirmed it. Nothing was soft about the man.

His lips were firm and well-shaped, not too full, but not thin. She wondered if they would feel cool because of the air temperature, or warm because of his body heat.

Unconsciously she licked her own lips, her eyes on his. Her own lips were cool. She wished suddenly that he'd kiss her so she could find out.

His hands gripped her arms hard through the layers of sweater and jacket as he stared down into her eyes. She felt a moment of panic, he hadn't read her mind, had he?

"Why are we hurrying?" she asked, catching her breath. "To make up for lost time from yesterday?" She would not fantasize about Hunter kissing her!

"To get ahead of the pack. You wanted to talk, start now. It won't be long before the others catch up." He released her and turned to start off again, the pace more leisurely. "And you might as well start with why on earth I should consider your firm for our account. We want a dependable company on which we can count to deliver what they promise."

"Jackson and Prince always delivers what we promise," she said, knowing his comment was a deliberate slur against her and her actions in the past. "Hunter, I'm sorry about the way our marriage ended. If I could do things over differently I would. I was horribly wrong in the way I handled things. I was distraught, my world had shifted and I felt guilty about the whole situation. That doesn't excuse the way I behaved, but I hope you will accept my apology. Please don't hold that against the company I represent. We have some exciting ideas for Trails West and I think it would be to your benefit to listen and consider what we have to offer."

"How does your family feel about your trying to get my account?" he asked.

"They don't know about our marriage," she said softly.

"What?" He stopped and turned to look at her. "What do you mean they don't know? Of course they do."

"I never told anyone."

"Your parents?"

She shook her head.

"I thought you said your father was angry about the marriage and that was why they refused to come to our wedding."

"He would have been," she said.

"Would have been had he known?"

"I tried to tell them at Christmas break how much I cared for you. They wouldn't listen. They insisted I forget all about that kind of nonsense and concentrate on my studies. They made sacrifices to send me to college and didn't want me wasting the money with such foolishness."

She blinked back unexpected tears. She'd tried to share life's most exciting aspect with her parents and they hadn't wanted to hear a word. Their idea of her future was ingrained and nothing could be allowed to interfere.

When the unthinkable had happened—when her father had been killed and her mother so desperately injured—she'd given up on her own dreams and hurried home to take charge. She sometimes wondered if it had been retribution for trying to have it all.

"Foolishness to fall in love and get married? Weren't they in love and married?"

"They'd had a hard time when first married. Education was important to them. They kept saying I needed to finish college before getting involved with anyone," she tried to explain.

"Only you didn't, did you?"

"Hunter, I can't change the past, I can only say sorry."

"A little too late."

They walked in silence for several moments. She remembered the tingling awareness she felt whenever she was around him, the shock of electricity when they touched. A dozen memories came to mind, each more special than the last. They'd been apart ten years, but it seemed like only moments. She didn't need complications like that. This whole journey was complication enough.

Heather had to ask.

"Is there any point in my continuing on this trek? Does Jackson and Prince have any chance at all in getting your company's business in the Pacific Northwest? Just tell me what you want me to do and I'll do my best. If it isn't good enough, well there won't be anything further I can do. I know you don't want me here, but neither do I want to be here. If I had known you would be on the hike, I wouldn't have come. Let's just get it over with!"

CHAPTER FOUR

HUNTER stopped, the question caught him by surprise. It shouldn't have. If he was adamant about not wanting to work with her, why should she subject herself to the rest of the week? From the looks of her, she was a hothouse flower who would never last the week in the wilderness to start with. In a way he was surprised she'd lasted this long.

Yet, he didn't want her to quit. What did that say about him?

"Quitting at the first sign of difficulty?" he asked, unwilling to make his decision based on past experience with Heather. He had not built Trails West into the growing and thriving concern by letting personal feelings interfere. He would be objective, listen to her presentation. If he truly thought her ideas best, then he'd have to see if he could work with the firm. The past was dead and gone. He had no feelings left for Heather—except perhaps anger.

"Not at all." Her chin came up and she tramped on.

He remembered her doing that in the past when things got difficult. She'd square her shoulders, raise her chin and charge ahead. Some things never changed.

What else had not changed? Did she still like hot chocolate before bed? Did she still tear up at sappy commercials on television? Was her way of doing laundry still whites, colors and then darks?

They'd dated for several months, married and lived together for three months. How much more he could have learned about her had they had longer? How much more difficult would it have been to forget her if they'd had longer?

Not that he had ever forgotten her. He'd learned that lesson well. His mother had bolted at the first crisis. Then Heather had left to return to her own family. Hunter had vowed after that to remain single and not get tied up with expectations that could never be. There was something wrong with him, obviously. Better never to count on a relationship than to be hurt again.

The trail grew steeper. If he remembered Alan's notes correctly, there was a switchback portion later that was steep and difficult, then an easy hike the rest of the way to the camp. There was even a fire lookout station not too distant from tonight's stopping point. He wondered if they should swing by and invite the ranger to join them for supper.

Checking his watch he calculated their chances of making the proposed campsite before dark. He'd like to get back on schedule, but wasn't sure the others in the group were up to moving faster. Especially Heather.

Though, to give her credit, she had kept up. Hadn't voiced a single complaint in his hearing.

"Hunter!"

He looked at Heather.

"Answer the question."

"Trails West will give serious consideration to the firms participating in this hike. More to those who finish. But ad plans and ideas play a major part of our decision." He stopped and looked at her. "Why don't you tell me about Jackson and Prince's ideas."

Heather was surprised at the invitation. She stepped closer wishing she could sit down somewhere and do nothing but talk about the campaign. Walking and talking would take a lot of breath and she'd have to watch where she was going. Still, this was her time, she had to make the most of it.

He glanced at her, but she never lifted her gaze above his throat, afraid to look into his eyes. The last time she'd stared into his, memories overwhelmed her. But he leaned closer. She could feel his breath swirl on her face, see the tiny pulse at the base of his throat. He was taller than she by several inches. His shoulders wide.

"Your lashes are natural." His comment was unexpected and she looked up involuntarily. Right into his eyes. For a second her heart stopped beating, then began pounding. She felt breathless and dizzy, as if the rest of the world was melting away. She was caught in his gaze, locked by his eyes, the pull of attraction almost magical. She had to look away or drown in his gaze.

It was almost a physical effort, but she broke contact, looking at the trail, across at the limited view.

"Of course they're natural, what did you think that I'd put on false ones on a backpacking trip? I don't even have any make-up with me."

"Some women won't go anywhere without putting on their face."

"I'm not one of them. What you see is just me," she snapped.

His hand reached for her chin, and gently turned her face up toward his.

"Look, this is a long trip and it won't be easy for either of us. I know we've got a past between us, but for this week, let's suspend the past. I can work on it if you can."

Nodding she agreed.

"I can tell you our marketing plans as we walk." She'd relish the activity—anything to keep from looking at Hunter and trying to concentrate on the ad campaign at the same time.

They started walking as she explained the concept she'd designed, she kept it impersonal, using the agency's name in place of her own. Given their past, she felt sure if he knew the ideas had originated with her, he'd summarily dismiss them from the running.

"Good plan," he said when she wound down.

Heather felt a flush of pleasure at his words. She thought the campaign was brilliant and knew it would open the way to great sales in her area of the country. She just hoped he'd meant it when he said he'd take the best ad plan.

Content she'd done the best she could, she began to relax. She watched Hunter as he walked along the trail. There was a definite air of competence and confidence that had not been so distinct ten years ago. He seemed larger than she remembered, but his honed, muscular body held not an inch of fat. His dark hair was tossed by the breeze, and she longed to touch it to see if she remembered the thickness.

Flushed, she looked away. She was not here to fantasize about her former husband, but to get the account for the agency. The responsibility seemed enormous when faced with the others on the trip. She was sure each agency had good, solid plans for Trails West. None of the others had a mark against them to start with. She knew the chances of Jackson and Prince getting the account were slim, but she'd go down fighting.

The trail skirted a bluff and the trees opened up, giving way to a spectacular distant view of rugged mountaintops and green tree-covered slopes. She stopped to take her fill of the vista.

"Hunter," she called as he continued.

When he turned to look at her, he frowned.

"What?"

"Can you get my camera out of my pack? I don't want to take it off and have to put it on again."

"We're not here on a photo shoot," he grumbled, but headed back. Glancing behind her he frowned again. "Where are the rest of them?"

"We charged ahead if you remember. I'm sure they'll be along in a moment. The camera is in the top outside flap." She turned and felt him zipping open the compartment. He handed her the camera.

"Don't take all day."

She nodded, focusing on the view. Pictures wouldn't do justice to the magnificence of the distant mountains, but they'd help her remember today, and how awe-inspired she felt seeing them like this. She'd never see a view like this from a car.

A few moments later Peter came round the bend of the trail and joined them.

"Where are the others?" Hunter asked.

"Bill's stopped at least a half-dozen times. He has the runs. John stayed with him, I came on." He looked at Heather and Hunter, obviously curious as to the results of her presentation. "Everything okay here?"

Hunter nodded.

"Are we taking a rest? I could go on for longer," Peter said.

"I wasn't planning to, but Heather wanted to take some photos. Might as well stop now and wait for Bill and John." Hunter shrugged out of his pack and dropped it on the side of the trail.

Heather snapped another photo, and then took off her pack. The relief was terrific. She hated to have to put it back on, but hoped she'd hide all feelings of that nature from her companions. She was enjoying the hike more than she expected, but it still wouldn't be her choice of a way to spend a vacation. Give her a lanai by the beach and room service every time!

"Did Bill eat something bad?" she asked. Everyone brought their own food, perhaps some of his food had spoiled.

"Don't know," Peter said. He turned to Hunter. "Ever do any hunting?" he asked. "I'm a deer man, myself." Without a word of encouragement, Peter launched into an account of his last hunting trip.

Heather moved away, hoping to escape the sound of his voice. She didn't hold with hunting anything. It was one thing if a person needed to eat, like early pioneers, or the native Americans. To kill an animal for sport was not something she supported. Maybe if the animals had guns, too, and had a fighting chance. She almost laughed at the mental image of Peter facing off against an armed deer. He had only to start talking, and he'd bore the animal to death.

She sat on the edge of a boulder and looked back at the two men. Hunter stood several inches taller, looked like he belonged to the rugged wilderness. Peter was gesturing as he got into his story. Hunter glanced around, fixing his gaze on her.

Heather wasn't sure, but she thought it held a beseeching look. Did he want to be rescued? The thought had scarcely taken hold when she rose and headed back to them. Maybe that was the clue she needed to get a chance for the account. Rescue him from Peter and she'd get extra points. Not enough to make up for the past, but maybe enough to open the door.

"Peter," she said when she joined them. "Sorry to interrupt, but I really don't like stories about dead animals. Tell me how you and your partners got started. I've heard of your company, of course, but don't know much about it except how successful it is. I'm sure Hunter would be interested as well." The magic words to Peter—Hunter would be interested.

It was as if she opened the floodgates. Peter was not a mite modest about the accomplishments of his firm, all due to his own brilliant expertise, of course. The company had started small, but was already one of the largest in Seattle with a new office in Portland. It continued to draw all the best firms, as fast as they could come up with ad campaigns for them.

Hunter watched in disbelief as Heather seemed to hang on Peter's every word. Was she really interested or just a consummate actress? Tuning out the man's bragging, he studied Heather. If he didn't know better, he'd think she'd deliberately come to rescue him from the man's boring hunting stories.

She flicked a glance at him, then resumed her gaze at Peter. The man could probably talk until dark without a break, but Hunter knew no one could listen that long.

John and Bill came up the trail. He looked at the two and headed for the man on the right. Bill was pale and walking with effort.

"We're taking a break. Sit down before you fall down," he told the man.

John helped Bill off with his pack. "He's in a bad way, Hunter. I think he should rest a while and drink a lot of fluids. He's getting dehydrated."

"What's the problem?"

"I feel sick as a dog," Bill said. He leaned against his pack, gazing dully across the view.

"Shall I call for an airlift out?" Hunter asked.

"Naw, don't bother. I'm sure I'll shake this soon."

"How long have you felt bad?" Hunter asked, hunkering down beside the man.

"Didn't feel that great when we started out, but I thought the fresh air would nip that. Yesterday was all right, but man I'm sick today." Bill replied, holding his abdomen. The man groaned.

Heather left Peter and hurried to the group.

"What's wrong?"

"Bill's sick. Stomach upset," John said.

"I have something for that," she said, hurrying to her backpack. She returned a moment later with some over-the-counter medication. "This should help with the symptoms," she said. "But if it continues a doctor may be needed."

Hunter rose. "I'm calling for medical assistance."

Bill groaned again. "Don't want to forfeit. I can ride it out."

"Hey, man, this isn't *Survivor.* The idea from marketing was to make sure everyone used our product, not some endurance test with the last man standing the winner."

"Or woman," Heather said.

Hunter gave her a look, but ignored the comment.

"You need help. Rest up and see how you feel. There's a fire lookout station not too far from here. Can you make it there, do you think? There'll be some way to get you out from there."

"I can make it. It comes and goes. I hate holding everyone up, though," Bill said.

"See how you feel after the medicine works," Heather said, patting his arm. "It might be all you need."

She sat beside the obviously distressed young man and wondered if the trip was jinxed. So far they'd lost Jess and now Bill was sick. That narrowed down the field. But if as Hunter said, it wasn't a case of who lasted the longest, maybe she should pack up and head out with Bill. She'd presented her plan. What more could she do?

Prove to Hunter she had what it took to be his account executive. The thought came suddenly. He didn't have a high regard for her. She would show him she was up to it. Get him to change his mind about her. Show him she was made of sterner material than he thought. Get him to like her.

She was struck by the last thought. Glancing at his profile as he talked to John and Bill, she wondered why she cared. If she could show him she'd changed since they were married, that she could be depended upon maybe the agency would have a shot at the account.

She'd let him down in the past, she knew. But her mother depended upon her and she had never let her down in ten years. Surely that should count for something.

How would Hunter view things if he knew the full extent of Heather's situation? She worked hard, then went home to care for her mother. It had been so difficult at first, but now she was in a routine. She hadn't wanted to tie him down. She knew how important getting an education had been to him. He had seen it as the only way to guard against fateful decisions of others that impacted family life.

She had feared his being tied with a wife who couldn't work because she had to care for her mother, and medical expenses for a dependent invalid mother-in-law would put an end to his education. She couldn't have allowed that to happen.

As the months had passed and he had done nothing to contact her, she'd known she'd done the right thing.

She blinked as tears formed. Knowing she'd done right was small consolation for the endless lonely years. She wished just for a moment that he'd stormed the house in Seattle and insisted they stay married, no matter what.

Hunter had not come. Their divorce had been handled quietly through impersonal attorneys. As far as Heather knew, no one in her family ever had an inkling that her heart had been broken by more than her father's death. She'd grieved for her father and her broken marriage at the same time.

A half hour later Bill declared he felt better. He thanked Hunter for the rest period. Thanked Heather for the pills. The group donned packs and headed out. Not surprising to Heather, Peter joined Hunter in the lead.

John smiled wryly. "If he doesn't get the account, it won't be for lack of trying," he said.

"I think he'll talk himself out of it," Heather said. "Can you imagine having to deal with him over the years?"

Bill smiled weakly. "No. But I'm not sure I'm making such a good showing."

"Hunter isn't going to judge you by your ability to not get sick," Heather said. The path began to wind upward. She'd be ready for camp when it came.

"How do you know that?" Bill asked.

"He said this wasn't a case of last man standing."

"Or woman," John said.

She nodded. "Exactly. Though when we return to the vehicles, I plan to be one of the ones walking out."

"Probably will be. But I'm not sure you're going to get the account," John said seriously.

"Why not?" Had others picked up on Hunter's animosity?

"I don't think Hunter's the type to mix business with pleasure."

"What does that mean?"

"If you saw the way he looks at you sometimes, you'd know he isn't interested in your ad campaign. I'd say he has a personal interest."

Heather was floored by John's assessment.

"Impossible!" she blurted out, astonished the man would think such a thing. If he knew their history, he'd know any staring Hunter was doing was with animosity, not interest.

Bill looked between the two of them. "You think?"

John nodded.

Heather shook her head and marched ahead. She debated whether to tell John the true nature of Hunter's feelings, but decided their personal business wasn't anyone else's.

Heather kept her camera handy and several times during the walk stopped to take photos. John and Bill passed her when she was trying to focus on a lovely delicate wildflower. Before she realized it, she was alone on the trail.

The silence was like nothing she'd known. She gazed around the forest, glad there was a definite path to follow. How did wilderness hikers manage if there were no trail? No wonder people got lost all the time when hiking.

"Heather!" Hunter came into view.

"What?" She stopped gazing and walked toward him.

"What are you doing? Keep up or I'll send you back with Bill. I can't afford to have you get lost."

"I knew enough to follow the path. I'm only a couple of minutes behind John and Bill."

"You're more than fifteen minutes from the rest of the group."

"I am?" Time went faster than she suspected.

He held out his hand for the camera. "I'll carry that. We don't have time for you to play around. The rest of us are waiting. Bill isn't doing well. I want to get to the fire lookout station and see if we can arrange transportation for him."

She tightened her grip on her camera. "I'll stop taking photos, but you don't get my camera."

His lips tightened, but Hunter lowered his hand and turned to start back the way he'd just come. "Very well, but from now on, you tell me when you want to stop. We'll either all stop, or you don't."

"Yes, sir!" She almost snapped a salute to his autocratic tone.

As she trudged along in silence, Heather had to acknowledge the wisdom of Hunter's edict. A person could become injured and separated from the group, causing untold delays. The trip had already been jinxed as far as she was concerned, first with Hunter showing up to lead the hike, then with Jess's injury and Bill's sickness.

Would he consider giving up and going by what he'd learned of the different agencies, or push forward?

Remembering how stubborn and determined her ex-husband had been, Heather knew Hunter would not give up.

When they reached the place where the others were resting, Heather slipped out of her backpack, stuffing her camera into the small outside pocket.

She went to sit beside Bill.

"Are you feeling any better?" she asked.

"I'm hanging in there," he said gamely.

Heather wasn't convinced. He looked slightly green and lapsed into self-contained silence when no one was speaking to him directly.

She looked at Hunter. He was watching her.

Rising, she crooked her finger at him and walked ahead a few paces.

He joined her.

"Bill's really not doing well," she said softly.

"I can see that. If he can make it to the lookout station, I plan to leave him there. With a road and transportation, he'll be able to get out to see a doctor."

"Are we going on?"

"You can leave with Bill if you like."

Heather put her fists on her hips, glaring at him. "I just wondered what the point is with people dropping like flies. First Jess, now Bill. It actually started with your marketing director. Maybe the hike is jinxed."

"Or maybe it's proving tougher than you thought with your fancy nails and city lifestyle. I told the group, I'm not judging solely on last man standing. If you want to leave, you've given me Jackson and Prince's presentation. I'll keep it in mind."

"Oh, like I'd get a fair hearing," she said sarcastically.

His eyes narrowed. "You're suggesting I wouldn't give the firm a fair hearing?"

"Darn straight I am. Tell me, Hunter, is there any chance in this world of your choosing the company I work for?"

He didn't answer immediately.

Heather's heart dropped. No matter the past, she had hoped he'd at least give their firm a chance.

"You could have another account executive," she said quickly.

"Early days, yet. Let's see what everyone is made of."

She sighed, knowing her best bet would probably be to cut her losses and leave when Bill did. But Hunter wasn't the only stubborn one in the group.

She turned and walked back to sit beside her backpack. There was another reason to stay. She was enjoying herself.

Heather had not had a vacation away from Seattle in all her adult life. Any time she took from work went to giving their apartment a thorough cleaning, replenishing linens and other accouterments of living, and taking her mother on day trips around the city.

She loved the serenity that filled her when she could be by herself enjoying all the wonders of the forest. It was nice to be alone with her own thoughts for a change.

If she were running the show, she'd return to that nice meadow by the stream and stay for the remaining four days. For the first time in ten years, tension faded. She could be herself here as no where else.

Maybe she'd join a hiking club when she returned home. Take a few trips during the year. She knew her mother would be a problem and have a trouble accepting her idea, but something could be worked out.

She looked over at Hunter, once again at the mercy of Peter's endless monologue. Did he go camping often? For a moment she let herself fantasize about the two of them taking quiet trips together. They'd walk in silence part of the way, sharing their delight in special vistas. At night they'd cook dinner, talk about the wonder of the day, and then crawl into a small tent and close the world out. She remembered their nights together.

He looked up and directly into Heather's eyes. She blinked and quickly looked away. He couldn't read minds, could he?

CHAPTER FIVE

THEY reached the fire lookout station in the early afternoon. The ranger agreed to get transportation for Bill and the others bid him farewell.

"I'd like to make the originally planned camp tonight, even if a bit late," Hunter said when the remaining members gathered round him. "It'll mean a quick pace, and few breaks, to make up for all the lost hours, but it's by a stream and is a known campsite. There will probably be other campers there, so we don't have to deal with only our own company."

"Let's do it!" Peter said.

"How late is late?" John asked.

"Before dark."

John nodded.

Heather had taken out some trail mix and reached back for her canteen. She wanted to be prepared for a long hike, and not be the one causing any delays.

Hunter looked at her.

"You up to this? You can still go with Bill."

"I'm going to walk out at the end of the hike to my

own car, and nail the account at the same time," she said holding his gaze.

For a moment she thought she saw a gleam—of amusement, or surprise?

Peter laughed. "Guess she's going on."

Hunter shrugged. "I suggest we send one tent back with Bill. That way, we'll be back to two tents, and can trade off carrying them equally." His look challenged.

Heather raised her chin. "Fine with me."

Before long they were off. John and Hunter carried the tents. Peter jockeyed for position next to Hunter, but he was soon sent to the rear so John could talk with the leader.

"Think you have a chance of making it?" Peter asked Heather.

"Of course, same as you." She didn't like Peter, but tried to mask her feelings to maintain harmony as much as possible.

"We'll see. I'm sure he likes the proposal I've discussed. We speak the same language. Nothing personal, but you and he aren't exactly simpatico."

If he only knew.

"We'll see, won't we?" she asked pleasantly, hoping he didn't want to talk the entire afternoon. She'd like to enjoy the brisk walk as long as she could.

Jess had been wrong. Today was the worst day of the hike, Heather thought a few hours later as she stumbled again. She was so tired she could fall sleep while walking. Her feet hurt. Her shoulders felt as if hot knives were piercing her. She was hungry and thirsty. How could she have thought hiking a fun vacation? She was in agony.

Hunter kept walking. John followed. Both of them

seemed as fresh as if they had just started, she thought grimly. Peter was flagging a little. She could tell by his silence. She had not thought anything could shut the man up. He didn't trip every third step as she did, but he was tired, too.

She wanted to ask how much farther, but refused to be the weak one in the group. She'd go down fighting every inch.

The sun was low in the western sky. If they didn't reach the camp soon, they would be in darkness.

Then she heard voices. Could they be near the campsite?

Up a slight rise, around a bend and there was a small creek. A campfire blazed near the bank, and three tents were scattered in the small clearing. Not as picturesque as the meadow had been, still it seemed like heaven to Heather's eyes.

Hunter spoke with the other campers, then chose a spot a short distance downstream from the others. He sent Peter for wood, and told Heather to get water.

She just stared at him, so tired she wondered if she could function.

"Need help getting out of that pack?" John asked softly.

She turned and nodded. "I'm so tired," she said.

"Me, too." He unbuckled her belt and slid the heavy backpack from her shoulders. "As soon as we eat, I'm for bed. Peter and Hunter can visit if they like, but I'm beat."

"Probably not, but your saying so helps," she said with a smile.

"Heather, are you going to get the water or flirt all night?" Hunter asked.

She turned and snatched the bucket from his outstretched hand without a word and walked to the stream. How dare he think she was flirting? She was merely being friendly with a fellow hiker.

Kneeling at the bank, she filled the bucket. Conscious of the warning not to drink the water without boiling it first, she let the coolness run over her fingers, imagining the icy water in her mouth.

Wearily she rose and returned to the fire Hunter had started. She held out the bucket, resisting the temptation to dump it over his head.

"For your information, I was not flirting. John helped me take off my backpack."

"Pull your own weight," Hunter said taking the bucket.

"Hey man, cut her some slack," John said, joining them with an armful of wood. "Her pack's as loaded as mine and she weighs about half what I do. Today's hike was a killer. I could have used some help myself."

Hunter looked at Heather. She looked exhausted. For a moment a pang hit him. Was he deliberately expecting more from her than the others? She was smaller than any of the others, and so far had done her full share. Was he looking for fault, for a reason to disqualify her, to turn down Jackson and Prince so he didn't have to see her again or have to work with her firm over the years ahead? She'd already offered another account executive if they got the job.

But he didn't want another account executive. He wanted to know more about Heather, how she worked, what her ideas were. How her life had turned out.

"It's okay, John. I expect after a good night's sleep, we'll all feel better," Heather said, ignoring Hunter. It rankled.

"Dinner first," Hunter said already thinking of a way to get Heather's attention.

She nodded and went to her pack for her food and cooking utensils. Peter joined them with another load of wood and sat down by the fire.

"Today was a killer hike. Good thing I'm wearing boots bought from Trails West, they kept me going when others would have had me whimpering by the trail."

Hunter shook his head. No matter what, Peter kept on pushing.

They shared the fire while preparing their meals, then sat on the ground to eat.

Heather looked thoughtful. Hunter wanted to ask what she was thinking. She didn't join in the conversations among them. Had she always been so quiet? He didn't remember that from before. They seemed to have endless things to say to each other every day. He had looked forward to breaks from study, to talk, kiss—

Don't go there, he warned himself.

"Someone give me a tent and I'll set it up," Heather said, scrapping the bottom of her bowl. "I'll be ready for bed in less than ten minutes."

"It's not even full dark yet," Peter said. "I thought we'd mingle with the others. Don't be a partypooper."

The other campers had been friendly and invited them over after they ate.

"You mingle, my ideal evening is to go to sleep," she said, unperturbed by his suggestion.

"I can set it up while you wash your utensils," Hunter said. He wondered if she anticipated sharing with him. Was that his reason for leaving the other tent behind? They weren't heavy, each of the men could have easily carried one. But this way, Heather was forced to share.

Maybe he'd learn a little more about her life since leaving him.

Not that he cared. But he had thought about her from time to time over the years and this would put closure on his speculation and curiosity.

Hunter went to set up their tent. By the time he finished she was there with her backpack already unzipped. She pulled out her ground cover and the sleeping bag.

"Nothing against your wonderful hiking boots, but I can't wait to get out of mine," she said, moving past him into the tent. He held the flap and watched as she quickly laid out her sleeping bag. She glanced over at him. The tent was dim in the fading daylight. The light from the fire didn't illuminate much. She looked soft and mysterious.

"Good night, Hunter," she said, reaching out to pull down the flap.

He rocked back on his heels. What he'd like to do is get his own gear and join her.

"Hey man, we going visiting?" Peter asked.

"Come on over," someone called from the other group.

Time enough to find out more about his ex-wife another night. It was too early to go to bed, and he had responsibilities to the others in his group.

Heather didn't even give a thought to her journal as she crawled into her sleeping bag. She'd try to jot some notes in the morning, but tonight she was too tired. It felt great to lie down. She closed her eyes, trying to remember the ideas that had played in her mind that afternoon—about different ways to use some of the camping gear she carried. Maybe play up the various angles. She also wanted to emphasize how helpful the clerks were to beginners. Did all of them have a different area of expertise? She'd have to check with Hunter.

How odd he'd thought she was flirting with John this evening. She had gone out of her way to stay away from the others. It was a luxury to be on her own, she wasn't going to get entangled with the competition. He didn't know her very well.

And who's fault was that? she asked herself just before she drifted off to sleep.

Heather woke to darkness. The air smelled fresh and clear, the soft sound of rain sounded on the tent. She turned over. Hunter's bulk was beside her, visible as a darker mass against the faint illumination from the campfire, burning low nearby.

"Go back to sleep," he murmured.

"It's raining."

"It'll put the fire out soon. I hope it stops before morning."

"I thought we were supposed to have nice weather."

"There was the possibility of showers." His voice was soft, familiar in the night.

"If it keeps raining, will we move on?"

"Have to see how things look. If it's just a sprinkle, no reason not to. If a downpour, we'd have to sit it out. You brought a poncho?"

She nodded, then answered realizing he couldn't see in the dark. "Yes. But it's at the bottom of my pack. I really didn't expect to use it."

"You'll have time in the morning to fish it out if you need it."

"Mmm." It was pleasant being warm and dry and listening to the gentle rain. And being with Hunter.

"Go back to sleep."

"What time is it?" she asked.

"About four."

She'd gone to bed before eight. No wonder she woke at the sound of the rain, she'd had enough sleep. Turning on her side, she let herself enjoy the sounds outside, the drips of the water from the trees, the soft soughing of the breeze. Soothing, she thought, drifting back to sleep.

The rain continued in the morning, a gentle drizzle. Hunter was up and gone by the time Heather awoke again. She dressed quickly, adding an extra long-sleeve shirt because of the damp, cool air. She found her poncho and pulled it out. Packing her gear, she donned the poncho and opened the tent flap.

Hunter was beside a roaring fire. John sipped coffee beside him. There was no sign of Peter. Heather took her own cooking equipment and walked to the fire.

"Coffee?" Hunter asked, lifting the pot from the flames.

She held out her cup and soon sipped the fragrant beverage.

The plastic rain gear covered her from head to well below her knees. Her hands got damp outside of the covering, but the rest of her stayed dry and warm.

"I take it this is still hiking weather," she said, watching others at the camp adjacent moving around preparing to depart.

"They are heading the same way we are and wanted to get an early start," Hunter said. "No rush for our part. Our next campsite is an easy day's hike away. As soon as Peter shows, we'll eat and head out. I'd just as soon get there and hole up in the tents rather than slosh around in mud."

"Fair-weather hiker?" Heather asked, feeling daring to be teasing him so.

"What about you, little hothouse flower? Anxious to spend the day in the rain?"

"Think how it will moisturize my skin," she retorted.

"You two have a history together," John said.

Heather and Hunter looked at him.

"I wasn't sure before, but now I am."

Heather looked at her coffee, unsure what to say.

"We were married in college, split after a few months. I haven't seen her in years before this," Hunter explained succinctly.

"Kept in touch?" John asked.

Heather shook her head. "It was a surprise seeing him on this trip."

"You didn't know he headed Trails West?"

"Yes, but I only learned that recently. I certainly didn't expect he would be on the hike."

"Thought you didn't keep track," Hunter said, his attention back on Heather.

She met his gaze quickly looking away. "I didn't know until I bought my stuff at the new Trails West store in Seattle. Your photograph is behind the main sales counter as one of the founders."

"So what do you think the chances are," John asked, "of such a thing happening? Must be fate."

Heather laughed. "I don't think so, unless it's an unkind fate." She shrugged, avoiding Hunter's gaze. "Sometime coincidences happen. This one is just more odd than others."

"Maybe," John said.

Peter emerged from his tent, frowning at the weather. "We going on?" he asked as he approached the fire.

"Any reason not to?" Hunter asked.

"Rain."

"Drizzle. If it gets worse, we'll stop, otherwise I want to push on," Hunter replied.

Peter was obviously a fair-weather hiker. He grumbled as he ate, and then packed up. The weather even had a dampening effect on his endless chatter. He trudged along the trail quiet as a mouse.

Heather relished the sounds and smells of the hike. Her face was wet, but the rest of her remained dry. It was colder than it had been, but with the layers of clothing she wore, she was comfortable and warm. As the day wore on, she decided she liked hiking in a light drizzle—especially if it kept Peter Howard quiet!

Hunter was just ahead of her and she watched him as she followed his lead. Was it fate that pushed them together again? She'd like to think so, but she really didn't buy that concept. If John were to be believed, it was time for second chances.

Second chances? Nothing had changed in her circumstances.

The changes had come in Hunter's life. He had his

college degree, had built up a flourishing company that was unlikely to end up closing as his father's factory had done. He was established.

Established enough to take on a wife and awkward mother-in-law? The thought came unbidden. Heather shivered at the idea.

She didn't even know if he was married. Nothing he'd said or done had led her to believe he had any personal interest in her. The contrary, in fact. He still seemed angry.

In the last ten years, he could have remarried and have a bunch of children. None of them had spoken of their personal lives.

She tried to picture him married. Jealousy pierced. It was stupid, she'd divorced him. She'd been the one to leave. Yet the thought of him with another woman hurt almost beyond bearing. She had never thought beyond their last day together. Time had not stood still for ten years. He would have moved on. As she should have.

By late morning the rain increased. Soon Heather needed to wipe her face occasionally to blot the rain. She looked around, but couldn't see much beyond the damp trees and the needle-strewn trail. The underbrush was thick, the carpet of pine needles beneath them was slippery with the damp. Pinecones were scattered around, some broken and chewed. She hadn't seen any animals, and if they had any sense, they'd be sheltered against the rain.

She wished she were.

When they reached a small clearing, Hunter stopped. "I think we'll hole up for a while."

"Good idea," John said.

"I brought cards," Peter said, "If we want to while away the afternoon, we could play a game or two of poker."

Heather shook her head. "You three play if you want. I don't play."

Hunter was already working to get their tent set up. John quickly started erecting the one he shared with Peter. When the tents were up, Hunter held the flap for Heather. She got out of her rain gear and crawled into the tent. It was cool, but dry. He followed her in, crowding her until she moved to the back wall.

"I'm not much for poker," he said, pulling his backpack in behind him. He zipped the flap closed and the two of them were cocooned in the small space.

"At least it's dry," she said, wiping her face with her sleeve.

"Colder today than yesterday," he said. He sat, leaned against his backpack and looked at her.

She stared back, wondering what she should say. All she had to tell him had been said. Now they were two strangers sharing a rainy afternoon.

"Are you married?" she asked, surprising herself. Waves of embarrassment flooded, but she didn't retract the question. She needed to know.

"Came close a couple of times, but never took the plunge again. After you left, and my mother's defection, I figured marriage isn't for me. Did you marry?"

She shook her head. "The reason I left our marriage hasn't changed. I have my mother to care for. What man wants to take on a wife and her mother?" She didn't have to tell him she rarely even dated—and then only to social events to further her career as her uncle saw it.

Hunter had come close a couple of times. That meant he'd really cared about at least two other women. How many others had he dated? She looked down at her hands, wishing she hadn't asked. It hurt to know life went on, and she had missed her chance at lasting happiness.

Hunter knew it would be a long afternoon. They'd been inside the tent less than three minutes and he already regretted stopping. He watched Heather, wondering what else two people who had once loved each other could say.

Her hair was wet, plastered to her face. Her cheeks were rosy from cold, and she looked tired. Had she looked that tired when he'd first seen her? Was the hike too much for her?

He longed to reach out and fluff up her hair, help her dry it so she wouldn't take a chill. Were they going to sit in silence until it grew dark enough to sleep? That was hours away.

He reached in his pack and pulled out his ground cover and sleeping bag. Might as well be comfortable.

"What are you doing?" she asked.

"Making my bed. I don't relish sitting on the hard ground all afternoon, and it's my guess the rain isn't going to ease up before dark."

He made short work of the process, putting his backpack near the flap and stretching out on the closed sleeping bag. Stacking his hands under his head, he stared up at the blue ceiling, thinking.

Heather hadn't married again. Nothing had changed,

from her perspective. How injured had her mother been? He hadn't been at the funeral because he'd been sitting his final exams. She'd insisted he stay and take them, finish the semester. She'd taken incompletes in all her courses to fly home to Seattle.

He had never met her parents. She had met his father at their wedding. The old man still asked after her sometimes. Hunter never had an answer for him.

He looked at Heather. She hadn't moved.

Reaching out, he tugged on her sleeve, slipped down to grasp her hand. "Put out your own sleeping bag, you'll be more comfortable."

Heather looked at him. His fingers felt hot against her cool skin, an electric pulse from his thumb struck straight to the center of her being. Her breathing stopped, she wondered if her heart had stopped. She'd never been so aware of another's touch, of the feelings and emotions churning within her. Of longings and regrets and desires washing through her.

His gaze dropped to her lips and Heather opened them slightly to take a breath. This was madness. She had better get control of herself.

She darted a quick look to his face, but his expression was neutral. She felt butterflies in her stomach at his touch, leaving her hand in his until he drew away, his fingers trailing slowly across the back of hers. She looked down at his hands, conscious of the heightened color in her face. She had always loved his touch, loved the feel of his strong hands on her. It had been too long since she'd been touched. Too long.

"Good idea," she said, pulling away and moving to open her pack and withdraw her ground cover, air mattress and sleeping bag. She inflated the narrow mattress and spread it and the sleeping bag on the tent floor as far from Hunter as she could—which meant about six inches. She reached in and pulled out some trail mix and her water bottle. Sitting at the foot of her sleeping bag, she munched on the trail mix.

"Lunch?" he asked.

"Yes. I don't see us building much of a fire in the rain."

"We will later."

"With wet wood?"

"There's always dry to be found if you know how to look for it."

She shrugged. Taking a sip of her water she looked at Hunter. It gave her a peculiar feeling. He was staring directly into her eyes, his own deep and fathomless. Blinking, she almost choked.

"Can I have a sip?"

She handed the bottle to him.

He took it and watched her closely as if divining her emotions when his lips touched the mouth of the canteen.

Heather almost groaned, as if she felt his warm lips touching hers. She turned away, anxious to leave, anxious to stop thinking about the man beside her. She was here on a mission. She needed to accomplish it and get out. Not let herself dwell on the disturbing man beside her.

He held out the canteen and she reached for it. His fingers brushed against hers, the contact surprising. She felt a jolt down to her toes. Her eyes flew to his, he felt it, too, if his startled expression was anything to go by.

Heather's heart pumped hard, there was a roaring in her ears, she was breathing as hard as she ever had on the trail. Was she going to faint?

The tent was too small. She needed air, space, distance from Hunter Braddock!

She was struck again at how masculine Hunter was, how suited for the rough and basic life outdoors, when compared with the other men she knew in the ad agency. She couldn't envision him in the boardroom of a corporation, yet knew he had to do well there, too, if Trails West and its success was anything to go by.

"This will be the longest rest period on our trip, might as well take advantage of it." He turned his gaze back to the ceiling of the tent and Heather began to relax.

She finished her snack and water, then drew her journal from the backpack and began to write.

"You are faithful to your diary every day," Hunter said a few moments later.

"It's a journal. I've never been camping before, so I want to capture everything. The scenery we've seen around here is as beautiful as any I've seen anywhere. I only wish it would open up so we could see distances. Anyway, my recordings will help when writing copy for camping gear, I think."

"What about other sports gear?" he asked. "Going to take up football or skiing?"

Looking at him thoughtfully, she tilted her head slightly. "I might—at least attend sporting events. If we get the account."

"There is that, isn't there?" His gaze was focused on her again.

"What?" she asked.

"You'd drive a saint crazy, Heather. I wanted to get in and get out with no complications on this trek. Why do you make it so damn hard?"

"I'm not doing anything!"

"You're you." With that he turned on his right side, giving her his back. Heather wrinkled her nose at his back and turned back to her journal. But the scenes from her morning walk wouldn't come. She could only think about Hunter.

The rain continued all afternoon. After writing as much as she could, Heather slipped into her sleeping bag. It was dim in the tent which made it difficult to see to write. She was still tired, and a little bored. Hunter seemed asleep, so she didn't even have him to talk with.

The melodious sound of the rain soothed her.

Hunter turned over. She looked at him, he was awake.

"I thought you were napping," she said.

"I did for a bit, but I'm not used to sleeping during the day." He rolled back on his back. "Did you sleep?"

"No. I was writing in my journal. I had an idea about brainstorming various ways your camping equipment might be used in addition to camping. Some of it's quite expensive, so if customers perceived more value than a few trips to the woods, they will be more inclined to purchase things."

"Interesting topic."

"We can expand it to other items beside camping gear."

"Like a kayak?"

She smiled. "Not unless someone wants it as a huge vase in their living room. But there have to be other things in the stores that have multiple uses if we think outside the box."

"Mmm."

"What if it keeps raining tomorrow?" she asked. "Will we stay again, or hike out despite the weather?"

"Giving up?" he asked.

"Just curious. I bet even John and Peter are wondering. You're quick to assign a feeling to me that isn't there."

"What do you expect?"

"I did what I thought was right."

"When?"

"Ten years ago, of course. Aren't we always talking about that? You didn't need the pressure and strain of a wife who couldn't work and a very dependent mother-in-law to boot. What if we'd stayed together? We had no money to speak of, and my mother's care took all the savings she and my dad had. We sold the house to make ends meet, found a small apartment and moved in when she was released from the rehab center. What about your plans for college and life? I couldn't let you change your life because of the accident."

He turned on his side, rising up on one elbow and looking at her in disbelief.

"You're saying you ended our marriage for me? Come on, Heather, your mother demanded you stay with her and you made your choice. It was clear, her or me, you chose her."

"My mother needed me."

"And I didn't?"

"No. I've never known anyone so self-sufficient. We

had great times together, I for one will always cherish the memories. But life isn't perfect. How could I turn my back on my mother when she needed me?"

"And now, does she still need you day and night now, Heather?"

"Yes."

"Come on, you said she's in a wheelchair. Millions of people function perfectly well on their own if they are that mobile. Plus there are health-care professionals who can help out when needed."

"You sound like my aunt Susan," she said.

"Who is Aunt Susan?"

"She's married to my uncle Saul, and she constantly tells me my mother is manipulating me, that she could manage on her own. But Susan doesn't live with Mother. She doesn't see how much she depends on me."

"How much?"

"What do you mean?"

"Are you there twenty-four hours a day? Obviously not, or you couldn't hold down a job, or come on this trip."

"I fix breakfast for us. I'm home in time for dinner each night, help her get ready for bed."

"And?"

"And what?"

"What else?"

"That's about it. On the weekends if she wants to go out, we go shopping or to the video store to rent movies. But she doesn't like to go out in public much, so we usually stay pretty close to home."

He lay back down. "It doesn't sound to me like she

If offer card is missing write to: The Harlequin Reader Service, 3010 Walden Ave., P.O. Box 1867, Buffalo, NY 14240-1867

BUSINESS REPLY MAIL

FIRST-CLASS MAIL   PERMIT NO. 717-003   BUFFALO, NY

POSTAGE WILL BE PAID BY ADDRESSEE

HARLEQUIN READER SERVICE
3010 WALDEN AVE
PO BOX 1867
BUFFALO NY 14240-9952

NO POSTAGE
NECESSARY
IF MAILED
IN THE
UNITED STATES

needs you. She can manage on her own all day and all night, just needs some help with meals and dressing."

Heather opened her mouth to contradict, then snapped it shut. Her mother did manage during the day.

"I'm all she has," she said quietly.

"Sounds to me like she needs to get a life. She must have friends. Doesn't she have any outside interests? What did she do before the accident?"

Heather looked at the ceiling of the tent, thinking back. Her mother had always been busy. Not always happily so, as she recalled.

"She did have friends. She worked part-time at a bakery near us. And then she was in the quilting club near our old house. She never sees those women."

"Why not?"

Heather wasn't sure. "The accident took a toll," she said. Why had her mother turned from her longtime friends? In the beginning, it was all she could do to get up and dressed. But as the months and years marched on, she had become proficient at dealing with day-to-day responsibilities.

The ones she took on. Could she do more? For the first time, Heather looked at the situation as Hunter must view it. As Aunt Susan tried to explain it.

"Maybe, but it was ten years ago. If she doesn't have a reason to push to get back her life, why bother? Sounds like she has it all her way. Any men in your life?" Hunter asked.

Heather shook her head. "I don't have much time to date."

"Mother wouldn't approve?" Hunter guessed.

She was silent. Her mother had complained on the few occasions she'd gone out on a date for fun. She wasn't as condemning if the date was business related, but insisted Heather be home in time to get her to bed.

"Or maybe you learned something from our marriage, and don't want to make that kind of commitment when you can't stick it out," he suggested.

"I told you, I thought I was doing the best for you. Do you think it was easy for me to walk away? I loved you, Hunter. I had the happiest time of my life when I knew you at college. I gave it all up to go home and deal with the aftermath of my father's death and my mother's injuries. Where do you get off condemning me? You never did anything to try to save our marriage!"

"I called and left a dozen messages. I came to Seattle one weekend, right after my finals were finished. Your uncle Saul sent me packing. He stated clearly that you didn't need any further complications, and it would be best if I stopped trying to contact you. His words exactly."

Heather sat up and looked at him, horrified. "That can't be. No one knew about our marriage."

He sat up and faced her. "Obviously Saul did. And I think your parents did as well. My guess is they were waiting until the end of the semester and would have forced the issue, but the accident happened instead. Saul handled your father's affairs after his death, right?"

"Yes."

"He knew the first time I called who I was. I think you need to find out if your parents knew or not. I'm betting on they did."

"I can't believe you tried to contact me and no one told me."

"Where were you those first few weeks?"

"Mostly at the hospital, or Aunt Susan would take me home to her place to rest. The funeral was hard. Not knowing if Mom was going to be okay was hard." She remembered crying herself to sleep many nights. The longing for Hunter's strong arms around her had been so intense she thought she'd die. The fear for her mother's life was the only thing that kept her from returning to Chicago and asking him for a second chance.

By the time she knew her mother would recover, the divorce papers had been served.

"This changes everything," she said.

"Doesn't change a thing as I see it," he replied. "Your family needed you and you left me to go to them. You made your choice. You didn't want us both."

"I didn't know you'd called."

"I wasn't playing some game where you leave and I chase after you. I wanted to know how you were, how your mother was. Instead I got the brush-off. You could have called me, you know. The telephone lines run both ways."

Hurt feelings had kept her from calling him. That and her determination to do what she thought was right.

She had explained it and it didn't make any difference to him. She'd left, and for that it looked as if Hunter would never forgive her.

"I did what I thought was right. Turned out great for you," she said. "You have your lovely company, a nice business going and obviously have no trouble finding other women for companionship. I'm sure you'll be able to find someone to have a family with and live together into old age."

He gave a harsh laugh. "Don't count on it. I'm not very trusting in that area these days."

CHAPTER SIX

"HEY in there." Peter's voice came from outside the tent. "You two awake?"

Hunter reached for the zipper and opened the flap. "What's up?"

"John has a large sheet of tarpaulin in the bottom of his backpack. We thought we'd try to rig up some cover and get a fire going. I don't want a cold dinner. What do you think?"

"I'll be there in two minutes." Hunter reached for his poncho and pulled it on. He left the tent, glad for the respite against the feelings he was discovering all over again about Heather. So her story was she left him for his own good.

That made him downright angry. Hadn't she given him any credit ten years ago to know what he could and couldn't handle? Or was that her bid for sympathy? Either way, it didn't work. He still believed when the chips were down, she left him behind. Just as his mother had done.

John was working on fastening a rope on one of the lower limbs of a nearby tree. The space beneath was open and fairly free of rocks and deadfall. Hunter grabbed another rope from a different corner and strung it to a tree. Peter picked up the third and before long the tarp was stretched out, with a downward slope on one edge to shed the water. The area covered wasn't more than eight feet square, but large enough for a fire and space for them to sit around it. At least there was no wind to blow the rain beneath the covering.

"Now to find enough wood to fuel the thing," Hunter said.

Heather joined the group. "I'll search for firewood, if you tell me how to find anything dry in this downpour."

"Look near the base of large heavily limbed trees, they shed the water away from the trunk," John said.

"Or beneath large piles of leaves. The top leaves sheet the water away and beneath that layer everything is often dry," Hunter added. He wished she'd stayed in the tent, but knew better than to suggest such a thing. It was bad enough John knew some of their history. He wasn't giving rise to speculation from any preferential treatment of Heather.

It was wet and dirty work finding enough dry material to build a fire that would last for several hours. Finally they had a good-size stack of wood.

"I wish we had a stream to wash in," Heather said, brushing her hands against each other trying to dislodge the dirt and crumbling leaves.

"Hold them up to the rain, they'll get clean soon enough," Peter grumbled.

She did so, then stepped beneath the tarp. She was cold. For the first time since she left the tent, water wasn't splashing on her face, however. If they had a fire soon enough that would warm her up, she'd be fine.

Hunter started the fire, feeding it slowly making sure it would take hold. Several moments passed before it was large enough to begin warming the air. He built it near the high edge of the tarp, to allow the smoke and heat to rise out of the lean-to. "Hot dinner tonight," Peter said with some satisfaction.

"We'll rig up something to catch the rainfall, then boil it," Hunter said. "At the rate it's coming down, we'll have enough to wash in as well as cook with by dinnertime."

Heather watched as Hunter took charge. Had he always been so knowledgeable and so able to lead men? She remembered being more interested in the two of them than in watching him with others.

She went back to the tent to get her cooking utensils and dried food. She would love something warm to take away the chill. She looked at her hands, dirty and cold. One nail was chipped. She had paid good money to splurge on the fake nails. Obviously they weren't designed for wilderness life.

Neither was she. She was cold, damp and uncomfortable. And confused with the feelings she was starting to notice around Hunter. She didn't want to be interested in the man. She'd run out of their marriage and nothing had changed. Her mother still needed her. She couldn't move to Denver even if Hunter asked her. She had done the right thing. She had to convince herself of that.

But what-if played in her mind. What if her mother could manage as Aunt Susan insisted. What if Hunter would give her another chance. What then? Would she take it?

"Heather? Bring my gear, will you?" Hunter called from the fire.

"Okay." She had seen which compartment he'd put his cooking gear when watching him pack yesterday. Gathering her things and his, she returned to the fire.

"I didn't know what you wanted to eat, so I brought a couple of choices," she said, handing him the packets.

His hand brushed against hers. Accidentally? The sparks that seemed to fly were surprising.

"Thanks."

He didn't look at her.

She sighed softly and moved closer to the fire. The warmth was heavenly. She wished she could just sit down by the fire and stay all night. She didn't belong here. The men were taking the awful weather in stride— except perhaps for Peter. He didn't like things not going his way. But John and Hunter relished pitting their wits against Mother Nature. And so far, they were holding their own.

She wished she was home. She'd never again take her warm apartment for granted when it was pouring down rain outside.

Did she have a chance to get the account? She was putting herself through a lot of misery for a slight hope.

Or was the hope for more than an account. Was it also a hope Hunter would view her defection in a different light? Stop being angry with her. And what? Be friends?

Eating a warm meal went a long way to balancing her mood, Heather found as she scraped the bottom of her bowl. She was warm, relatively dry and content to listen to the desultory conversation of the men. If she paid a bit more attention to Hunter when he spoke, that was natural. He was the one who had the power to grant the account.

Looking around the tight group at the fire, she wondered how she'd decide if the choice was given to her. Of course, she'd choose Jackson and Prince, but if that was up in the air, she thought she'd go with John. She could see working with him for years into the future, building a media campaign that would make Trails West a household word in the Northwest.

Jackson and Prince could do that as well.

She could do that, if Hunter would give her the chance. And make it more meaningful for him than any of the competition. She owed him big time and would work tirelessly to give the best she had.

And he'd never think it enough.

Depressed at the thought, she reached for the boiling pot of water and rinsed her bowl and pan, using the water sparingly.

"Any thoughts about tomorrow?" she asked.

"If the rain stops, we'll go on," Hunter said.

"If it drops to a drizzle, we could go on," John said. "I've hiked in worse."

"Me, too," Peter quickly added. He looked at Heather. "But not all of us have."

"I can go anywhere you go, Peter," she said quietly.

Looking at Hunter, she was surprised to find he was looking at her, with speculation in his gaze.

The next morning the rain had stopped. It continued overcast and gray, with the trees dripping moisture.

After breakfast, they broke camp and headed out. Peter once again joined Hunter.

"Interesting how he thinks annoying Hunter will win him the account," John said pleasantly as they walked side by side a few feet behind the other two.

Heather laughed softly. "Maybe he can't recognize he's annoying him."

"Maybe. Tell me a bit more about Jackson and Prince. I know Saul Jackson, of course. We meet at Chamber of Commerce functions."

"It's a family business for the most part, but that doesn't mean we aren't really good. I've been there almost nine years." For a moment the number seemed daunting. She had so wanted to be a teacher. Instead circumstances had dictated otherwise and now she spent her days dreaming up ads to sell products to the public. And they didn't even represent a toy company or game firm. Except for holidays when she saw some of her cousins's children, she was never around kids.

"You do have a good reputation in Seattle. Saul is a man of his word."

"He's my uncle, and has been wonderful to me. Tell me about Statton Brothers. I know you are one of the largest on the West Coast, with offices also in Portland."

The time passed pleasantly as they walked. John was entertaining and more than once Heather laughed at his comments.

When they stopped for a break, Hunter glared at her.

"I take it you are enjoying yourself," he said when the others were busy taking off backpacks.

"I am. Aren't I supposed to?" she countered.

"Walk with me on the next stage, I want to hear more about Jackson and Prince," he ordered.

She watched him walk away and almost snapped a salute to his dictatorial tone. But the entire purpose of the trip was to sell Jackson and Prince. It looked as if Hunter was going to keep an open mind.

Heather marched purposely beside him, telling him about the agency, their glowing record of boosting sales for firms who hired them. She glossed over some of the recent lost accounts. In some instances companies changed ad agencies as often as their owners changed socks.

He listened to her but said little. She watched him, trying to judge his thoughts. She was being as businesslike as she knew how, but her real interest lay in knowing more about what Hunter had done over the past ten years. She knew he'd built a successful business. And come close to marriage again.

Did he ever think about what they might have had? Ever wish they could start over, making allowances for her mother? Of course, he hadn't. She'd made that clear when she left, she wanted nothing to do with him again. It had seemed so right at the time. But circumstances had changed over the years. She had a job that could support her mother. Hunter had made a success of his life. If they got together now, things would be so different.

Conversation slowed as they walked. She looked around, taking note of the beauty of the forest. The woods looked as if man had never set foot in them before. The trees grew tall and stately, untouched by lumbermen and their saws. The undergrowth was sparse, the trees shading the forest floor so that little vegetation grew on the steep hillside.

Heather enjoyed the pristine, peaceful setting. She let her mind wander, and found it going back to Hunter time and time again.

Hunter had moved ahead and she lengthened her stride to keep up. She wanted to offer no reason for complaints from him, and refused to give him any openings for more sarcastic remarks. They hurt. She wanted him to think kindly about her.

Every now and then Hunter would glance up and survey the area, looking at the view, such as it was. Heather would always follow his gaze and drink in the setting. Primarily, however, she had to watch where she was stepping. The terrain was uneven and rock-strewn. The squishing of their boots on the wet needles was the only muffled sound. Even Peter had grown silent. Or was it not worth the time to talk to John when Peter's main goal was convincing Hunter his agency was best.

Heather watched Hunter as he took long strides, moving as effortlessly through the forest as if he were on a deserted city street. It wasn't fair. Her pack was heavy and she was again growing tired. She pushed back her sleeve to check the time. They'd been walking almost an hour since their break. It would not be dark for another several hours. Another bend, and the trail dropped. Once they had to jump down a couple of feet where a slipout had obliterated the faint path. Another bend. This time Hunter stopped. Before them lay a creek. The water splashed and dropped over the rocks strewn throughout. It was fifteen feet wide with no clear way across. This was not a narrow creek like they'd crossed before.

"No bridge?" she asked, a sinking feeling in her as she already knew the answer.

Peter and John joined them. Peter gave a low whistle.

"We'll have to cross on the rocks," Hunter said, studying the water swirling around boulders in the stream bed.

"How?" Heather asked, looking at the foaming water in horror. "There isn't a single rock that isn't covered by the water. I don't want wet feet the rest of the day, I'd freeze. Or worse, fall in."

"We'll fan out. Peter, you and John go that way, Heather come with me. We'll look for a safer place to cross." He moved upstream, studying the rushing water, seeking a way to cross safely.

Heather watched him for a minute in exasperation. She followed, also looking for a place to cross where she wouldn't get drenched. It was noticeably colder now, as the afternoon waned. The damp from the earlier rain penetrated and chilled her to the bone. She wanted to start walking again, at least that kept her warm.

"Heather, over here," he called.

Joining Hunter at the edge, she looked at the creek. Here and there rocks thrust up, some flat, some round. All were wet, from the stream or the rain, she couldn't tell. One or two had a thin sheet of water covering them.

"They'll be slippery. But I don't want to go any farther from the trail than we need to. If we cross, we'll head downstream to find the others and they can come back here."

She didn't like the looks of it, but she wasn't likely to find a better spot. If he thought it their best shot, it probably was. It was not deep water, worse case would be she'd get her feet wet, but wouldn't drown. "Do you go first or me?"

"You go first. I'll follow and be able to help if you fall."

She glanced at him to see if he was being sarcastic, but his expression seemed innocent. The crossing was either more treacherous than it looked, or he didn't have a high confidence in her ability to cross.

She studied the rocks, trying to fix them in her mind so she could make it across as easily as possible.

Hunter leaned forward, his face near hers, pointing with his left hand. "Start here, then try that one there. The third one is washed by the stream, but not enough to cover your boots, I think. Don't stay on it long and the water won't penetrate your waterproofing."

She tried to follow his explanation, look where he was pointing, but was overwhelmingly conscious of his nearness, the warmth emanating from his skin, the gently velvet tones of his deep voice. He was so close she had only to turn her face and she would bump heads. Or their mouths would connect and...

She forced herself to concentrate on what he was saying.

"...then you're home free."

"Here goes nothing," she mumbled wishing she had not been so distracted. Wishing he'd continue to hold her shoulder, and point out things she should look for. She liked the feeling of his hand, the sure tone of his voice. Long buried memories rose. She fought them back. She had to get across the stream, not wander down memory lane.

She stepped out on the rock. Had she not had the backpack throwing off her balance, she would not have thought much about crossing. But the extra weight made the crossing more difficult.

She stepped on the submerged rock, her foot slipping a little. Recovering, she jumped to the large flat rock that was next. It teetered, slowly moving beneath her feet. Fear struck her that she would end up in the cold creek after all.

Gritting her teeth, she ran across the next three rocks and jumped for the far shore. Her heel squished in the mud at the edge and she scrambled farther up, throwing herself forward to counter the weight of the pack. She landed on her knees, but she made it!

A smile of satisfaction lit her face as she turned to Hunter, still across the stream. "I did it!" she called excitedly.

"Good job. You knocked the flat rock over, though, so I'll have to try a different route."

But he didn't look for another route, he kept staring across the water at her. The minutes ticked by slowly as the smile began to fade from her face, and her heart began pounding. Heather could feel the pull of attraction even across the rushing stream. The heat rose in her face, spread through her body. She no longer felt cool. She had to look away before he consumed her. She broke contact, dropping her eyes to scan the water. Where would he cross?

* * *

Hunter moved upstream a few yards and started across. Twice the rocks beneath his feet moved, once his foot was totally submerged, but in only seconds he was on the same shore. He walked slowly down to where she was waiting feeling as if he'd been kicked in the stomach. He had no business staring at her, but she'd looked so excited having accomplished the crossing. Her eyes sparkled, her smile was radiant. God, she was beautiful.

"Good job. No problem, right?" Hunter smiled, his hands tightening on her arms. Slowly he lowered his head and lightly touched her lips. As Heather moved to step closer, Hunter broke the kiss, holding her a moment to make sure she was steady on her feet. Without another word, he motioned downstream. She no longer belonged to him. He dare not forget that.

"Let's find the others and get moving. We've a little time left before we need to make camp."

He was a fool for continuing. When Jess fell or when Bill got sick, he should have canceled the hike. He was perfectly content judging the new agency based on the work submitted, which clicked with his and Trevor's ideas for their company.

But he'd kept going. And he knew it was because of Heather. He needed to get his head on straight. She'd left him years ago. Spending a few days in the mountains together wasn't going to change things. He had moved on, so had she.

Instead of calling off the trip, however, he continued. And was looking forward to spending the night in the same space as Heather tonight and tomorrow night. It was quiet torture, breathing in her sweet scent, and not touching her. Knowing she was inches away and refraining from taking her into his arms. Remembering all the days and nights they'd made love when they'd been married.

"You made it across," Peter called from the opposite shore. The stream had deepened, the banks narrowed.

"I think we can jump it," he said.

"Don't risk it," Hunter said, shrugging out of his pack. "We found a spot upstream a little way that's perfect." He put his backpack on the ground next to Heather. "Watch that for me. I'll travel faster without it."

He returned to the crossing spot, talking across the stream to John and Peter as they retraced their steps and continued to the crossing.

Being alone in their tent wasn't the only torture, he thought as Peter joined him, exulting in his prowess at crossing. The man would drive a saint crazy. But if he had to put up with him to continue with Heather, he'd do it. The hike was ending in three more days. They'd go their separate ways and likely never see each other again.

The thought definitely didn't sit well with Hunter.

Heather sat down beside the two backpacks. She watched Hunter walk back upstream and closed her eyes and let the magic moment of that kiss wash through her. It had been friendly, not at all like the ones he'd given her in the past, hot and passionate. But she savored his touch, the clean pine scent around them, the cascading water behind her. The feel of his mouth against hers, his body sheltering hers. It wasn't enough. She wanted more.

All too soon they were on the way again. Hunter kept Heather with him with John and Peter following.

She looked at him as much as she could as they walked along, drinking in the sight of his tall presence, the easy way he handled the hike. She was impressed with the man he'd become. Wished she'd had a part in his life. If Jackson and Prince got the account, would they see each other from time to time? Or would he take her suggestion to get another account executive? She wished now that she'd never voiced that idea.

The trail began to rise steeply once they left the stream behind. Hunter pushed forward, stopping to search from time to time for the easiest way to proceed. Reaching back to help her, his warm hand grasped hers, sending tingling pulses of electricity up her arm, through her whole body. She never wanted him to let her go, yet, practically snatched her hands away as soon as she could manage on her own. Aware of Hunter's cool regard each time, she became more and more flustered as the climb went on.

At a particularly steep area, he took her hand again. He said nothing as they walked along, rubbing gently the softness of her skin. Her hand felt small in his, and Heather felt an unfamiliar warmth rise in her.

Heather glanced at Hunter from beneath her lashes, but his eyes were on the trail, his thoughts obviously elsewhere. The comfortable feeling she had with his hand holding hers faded and an awareness of something more arose. Obviously he didn't feel the same pull of attraction. She was in this alone. How pathetic. If she thought she could make him fall in love with her again, give them both a second chance, she was obviously in a dreamworld.

Her fingers tingled in the firmness of his hand, with the feel of his skin against hers, the warmth he generated. His palm and fingers were calloused and hard against her own. Heather didn't want comfort from him, she wanted more, much more. She could spend a lifetime with this man. Always know she was safe and secure. What would it be like to share a life with him, to be loved, cherished and taken care of? What if the accident had never happened. Or if her mother had not been so badly injured?

Her body longed for his. For the long and loving nights he'd given, the hot, passionate embraces that could cause her soul to sing and her life to explode into shining happiness. She longed to meet him again as an equal in the delights of love. To erase those lost years.

She yearned for an uncomplicated life. That they could have met without all the complications that now engulfed them. She stumbled on the path, almost stopping to tell she wanted another chance. See if she could change their headlong rush to farewell.

She was falling in love again. And with a man who didn't even like her this time around! How ironic, she'd walked away, now was trying desperately to think of a way to have what she'd thrown away. She peeked at him again. Was there any feeling for her, other that exasperation at being saddled with her for the trip?

They broke for a late lunch then resumed, Peter once again with Hunter.

"You should have had a turn in the front," Heather told John.

"I'll get my turn, don't worry. Be interesting to see at the end of the trip who comes out with the account."

"I hope it's you," she said, watching the two men ahead of her disappear around a bend.

"Not your agency?" John asked.

"I don't think we have a chance."

"Want to talk about it?" he offered.

"No. Not really. There's nothing to be done."

"My wife says I'm a good listener," John said.

She smiled sadly. "You're lucky to have a wife who thinks that. I remember my mother always telling my father he never listened to her."

"Some men don't."

"Neither one of them listened to me."

"Sometimes parents don't listen, either."

"They treated me as if I were a baby," she said, remembering the frustration of that Christmas visit. She was in love, the forever kind that had changed her life, and they pooh-poohed the idea, telling her over and over her studies were more important than some passing fancy in some young man.

"You're an only child, is my guess," John said.

Heather nodded.

"Tough being an only, I always thought. No one to take the limelight but you. No one to share responsibilities with. Lots of difficulty being the only one."

"I had thought to have a houseful of kids. Now I'm not even married, and not likely to get married. So much for all those babies I wanted."

Heather stopped and looked at John in dismay. "I'm sorry. I don't know why I said that. You certainly aren't interested in my life. You're here for the Trails West account. Forget I said anything."

"What happened between you and Hunter?" he asked.

She resumed walking, debating whether to tell him the entire story or not. It really wasn't any business of anyone but Hunter, but she had never been able to talk about her marriage, and the painful parting. After this trek it was unlikely she'd ever run into John again.

"My dad was killed and my mother injured very badly. I left him to go home to care for my mother. I thought it was the best thing at the time. He still had to finish college, make his way in the world. He didn't come from money, so it was a struggle to make ends meet when we were both students. I knew he would give up college to support me and my mother and I couldn't bear the thought of that. It was too unfair. So I left."

"I'm sorry about your father. Is your mother all right now?"

She shook her head. "She's in a wheelchair, and still suffers a lot."

John didn't say anything, but Heather suspected he was able to put two and two together.

"I didn't expect to see Hunter on this trip," she said quickly. "I only took over the proposal at the last moment. It was when I was buying my camping gear at the Seattle Trails West that I learned he was the founder of the company. I never expected him on the trip."

"A surprise for both of you," he said. "Or maybe, fate's way of giving you another chance together."

She closed her eyes against the hope that burst forth. Would it be possible?

"I don't think so," she said, not wishing to hope for the moon. "My mother is still dependent on me."

"But nothing else is the same," John said. "And I suspect Hunter makes enough to support you and your mother now."

"Oh, how awful. I couldn't go back to him now, just as if he were a meal ticket. I hadn't thought about that aspect. We can never get back together as long as I have my mother!"

She would never let Hunter think she looked on him as a meal ticket. She supported herself and her mother just fine. If things changed and her mother became self-sufficient...

Who was she kidding? Her mother wasn't self-sufficient and probably never would be. Other than her spinal cord injury, she was healthy and likely to live another forty years or more. A lifetime.

"Then maybe it's time to think of an alternative living arrangement for your mother," John said.

Heather shook her head. She had to stay with her. Her mother had no one else.

CHAPTER SEVEN

HUNTER called a halt to the day's hike early at a small clearing next to a creek. Soon a fire was roaring, taking away the dampness of the air. The rain had held off, but it remained overcast.

After an early dinner, the hikers sat around the fire, sipping coffee and talking.

Heather contributed little to the conversation. She was thinking about what John had said about second chances. And the different circumstances in her life and in Hunter's. Could something be worked out? Her aunt Susan had said for years there was nothing wrong with Amelia but her dependency on Heather. She hadn't minded taking care of her mother—at first. But in all honesty, Heather had chaffed at the situation lately. She was still young, still wanted to marry and have a family. How could she do that when her mother was so demanding. Heather was happy to support her—but was her mother taking advantage?

When she thought about the past years, she had to acknowledge that her mother did nothing to encourage her to date, to find a mate. Whenever Heather did go out for fun, her mother made sure she knew to be home before Amelia would consider going to bed.

Heather wondered how her mother was faring this week. Aunt Susan would most likely do as little as possible for her sister-in-law. Could her mother cope, or was she in dire straits with Heather gone?

She wished she could borrow Hunter's cell phone and call her aunt to check.

Jumping up, she brushed off the seat of her jeans and looked at the men who had turned to stare at her when she rose.

"I'm going for a walk."

"We've been walking all day," Peter said.

"I know, but this'll be fun, without the heavy weight of the backpack. There's some sunshine beneath the clouds, so I'm hoping for a spectacular sunset."

She turned and walked downstream slowly, studying the weak rays from the setting sun. The cloud cover didn't reach the horizon and there were faint beams from the sun.

"You holding up all right?" Hunter asked behind her.

She turned. They were no longer in sight of the campfire. The light was fading as the day waned.

"I'm doing fine, thank you."

"I think so, too," he said.

She felt flustered. "Oh?"

"I didn't think you'd make it this far when I saw you at the lodge." He walked past her and ambled along the stream.

Heather quickly followed, catching up in only a few steps. "I told you I would."

He nodded.

"Jackson and Prince would do a great job for Trails West," she said.

"Probably."

"We have a good campaign and—"

He stopped and turned to her. "I don't want to talk, Heather. Just enjoy the view. I often thought we should go camping. Had hoped to find a few weekends that summer after school, but you left instead. You were once everything a man could ever want in a woman."

Before Heather could utter a sound, Hunter bent his head and captured her lips. His arms pulled her to him, firm across her back, his chest hard as he molded her to him, his mouth sweetness and passion. A slow spreading warmth began deep within her, moving to engulf her whole being. His mouth moved against hers, demanding and then receiving an equal response.

Heather was caught in the enticing sensations Hunter evoked. It was exhilarating, fantastic, erotic. His lips were hot, provocative, now teasing hers, now raising desires long dormant. Filling her with sensations she'd not felt in ten long years.

She had to respond, the driving need rose from the very core of her being. She had to give all he wanted, all she had to offer. She rubbed against him, wanting more.

His tongue moved to taste the sweetness of her, the soft skin of her inner lip, the smooth hardness of her teeth, plunging to dance with her own tongue, withdrawing to invite her into his mouth.

His arms tightened, Heather cradled his head, her fingers lost in the thick springiness of his hair, the strength of his shoulders. The remembered feel of his skin swept through her. The soft flannel of his shirt added to the warmth her fingers encountered. His soft stubble heightened the sensations around her mouth. Her senses were sharpened, everything she touched caused new wonder, new delights, old memories.

The flame began deep within her, her heart filled with a strong longing, her breath came in gasps. The feel of his hair, his skin, fed the longing, fed the growing desire. The feel of his hard body against hers exploded erotic images behind her closed eyes. How could she ever have left this man? How could she go on without him?

He moved his hands to cradle her head, tilt it back, seeking the soft vulnerability of her throat. Hot kisses had her trembling with weakness and yearning. Again and again he kissed the pulsating base, his lips warm against her flushed skin.

"Hunter," she murmured. Ten years apart vanished in an instant. It was as if they were still married, still in love, still the only two people on the earth.

Her voice ended the madness. He slowly withdrew, breathing unevenly, his hands growing harder as he pushed her away. His eyes glittered in the faint light, his voice was ragged.

"This will never work. Go back to camp."

He turned abruptly and walked into the twilight.

She stood, trembling, and watched him walk away in disbelief. Her legs could scarcely hold her upright. The fire flamed in her cheeks now. What an idiot she was. She watched for long moments, hoping he'd return, willing him to come back. Finally admitting defeat, she turned to stumble back to camp and to the tent he'd already erected.

Her body ached with longing. She felt doubly lonely and sad after the passion of that kiss. They connected as she had never felt with another soul. She wanted him every way a woman wanted a man.

She knew he was not unaffected by her presence. He had kissed her several times. Several heavenly stolen moments of delight. Would he ever give them another chance? Would he ever consider they'd been given a second chance and work to make the most of that opportunity before it was too late?

What could she do to show him she had matured and changed? For a moment she ruthlessly consigned her mother to her own devices. Putting herself first, for the first time in a decade. She'd give up her job, her home, everything if Hunter would invite her back to Denver.

Startled at her thoughts, Heather tried to blank out her mind as she got ready for bed. Snuggled in the sleeping bag a few moments later, those thoughts rose once more.

Was there anything she could do to encourage Hunter to try again?

Before she came up with an answer, she drifted to sleep, alone in the two-man tent.

When Heather awoke the next morning, she was still alone in the tent. Had Hunter come in late and left early? Or stayed elsewhere last night.

She dressed swiftly and headed out to the campsite. She was nervous leaving the tent, very conscious of last night and how she had felt after his kiss. Hoping she looked more composed than she felt, she bravely moved out to sit by the fire. John and Hunter were already drinking coffee. Peter was not there. Heather greeted them and poured herself a cup of hot coffee. She noticed Hunter avoided looking directly at her. If he wanted to ignore her, fine. But her heart ached at the thought. The memory of that explosive passion warmed her even as she sat on the small mat. The bittersweet memory would not be banished and in the long days of the future, she'd think of this trip and the love that bloomed again.

Love. She was in love with Hunter. Had always been though she'd tried to deny it, tried to go on with her life as she had chosen it so long ago.

She looked at him, wishing with an intensity that was fierce, that he could love her. People didn't do what other people wanted just because they wished it, however. She had no doubt once he was back in Denver, he'd quickly forget their brief kiss and resume his life— without her.

By the time Peter joined them, breakfast was almost made. Once finished, Heather decided she would have to put the foolish dreams away. She'd treat Hunter as impersonally as he wanted, and hope the remaining days sped by. She'd try to treat him as if they'd never met before this trip.

Her tongue traced her lips, remembering his kisses, the very taste of the man. Would he ever kiss her again? Ever in love, not in anger? She closed her eyes, feeling again the strength of his arms around her, the hardness of his chest when he drew her against him. The deep velvet tones of his voice.

"You okay?" Hunter's voice broke into her dreaming.

Opening her eyes, Heather focused on him, nodding. His face gave nothing away.

"I'm fine. I'll pack up my stuff and be ready to go."

She left the fire before she blurted something out that would embarrass them both.

Hunter watched Heather enter their small tent. The one he'd left before dawn to escape the scent of the woman sleeping beside him. She always smelled like some fragrant wildflower, a light sweet scent. He'd not been able to sleep last night for thoughts of the kiss they'd shared. He'd wanted to draw her into his arms, kiss her senseless and make love to her until dawn.

Instead, he'd tossed and turned until he finally awoke before daylight and had come out to build the fire. Several cups of coffee had done nothing to assuage the longings he had. He wished she had not come on the hike.

Or did he? He had moved on after she left. He had made a life for himself and rarely thought about Heather these days. But she had never completely faded from his mind. Sometimes when he was lonely, he remembered her laughter. Sometimes when he felt tired to the bone, he'd remember their nights together. It had been hard to move on without her. He'd thought when they were in college that they'd be together forever.

Now the only tie they had was a tenuous one centered around business—if he selected Jackson and Prince as the ad agency in Seattle. Would that be the stupidest thing he could do or what? What they had burned out long ago. She'd chosen a different family, a different life. He'd be a fool to pursue the thought of renewed contact changing anything.

But he still wanted her.

"The weather looks good," Peter said, interrupting Hunter's thoughts.

"The sky is clear, a good sign. Today should have some of the prettiest views we'll see." In two more days they'd be back at the lodge and go on their separate ways. He was counting the hours.

"Tomorrow is the last day," John said. "It's been a good trip, Hunter. Even if we don't get the account, I'm glad I came on the hike."

"Will you be awarding the account when we reach the parking lot?" Peter asked. "Or wait until Monday morning? If you're staying in Seattle over the weekend, you're welcome to use the company's condo. We keep it for visiting clients and friends."

"Alan will be the one awarding the account," Hunter said. "I'm returning home as soon as we finish the hike."

Heather could hear the conversation from the tent. She clearly heard Hunter. Had he raised his voice to make sure she knew he couldn't wait to return to Denver?

She tried not to let it matter, but suddenly she had the urge to cry. They had been so in love, so sure their future would be wonderful together. Instead they'd only had a few months and she'd left.

She sat on the floor of the tent, leaning against her backpack, trying to think. What if she found work in Denver? What if she could find live-in help for her mother? Would Hunter be at all interested in taking up with her again once she got her life in order? Or was it far too late?

Why should he forgive her? She'd broken her vow to cling to her husband. Could he ever trust her loyalty again? But they were in different places now. She had a job and experience. She had a marketable skill that would help in finding work.

Nothing like the position he held, however. No matter how she looked at it, she couldn't bring herself to suggest they start seeing each other. It smacked too much like latching on after he'd done so well. She would never let him think of her as a gold digger.

Hunter lifted the flap and looked at her. "Ready to go? I want to pack the tent."

"Ready." She pulled her backpack out and before she could turn to help, Hunter began disassembling the tent. In only moments he had it securely affixed to his own pack.

They left in single-file order, walking quietly along the almost silent trail. Even Peter seemed talked out, for which Heather was grateful. She was tired of hearing his voice drone on and on.

The scenery was spectacular, just as promised. There were many open areas that gave way to panoramic views of tree-covered mountains soaring against a blue sky. Skirting a meadow they saw a small herd of deer feeding. Holding still for endless moments, she enjoyed watching the animals graze, lifting their heads from time to time to search for danger.

Hunter moved quietly to her side and unzipped her outer pocket, reaching inside for the camera. "You'll want this," he said softly.

She nodded, touched he'd come without asking. She snapped several shots of the beautiful animals before they darted away.

"How did you manage that?" Peter asked jokingly.

"Just part of Trails West's service," Hunter replied in turn.

"What do you plan to do with all the pictures you've taken, Heather?" John asked.

"Use them in ads for Trails West, of course," she replied throwing a challenging look at Hunter. "Nothing like firsthand experience, right?"

He said nothing, but turned to start walking again.

She hadn't expected him to confirm or deny her agency's chances at the account, but she wanted him to know she still was in the running. Maybe there was a chance he wouldn't dismiss their account out of hand because of their past. She hoped he'd be that fair, no matter the personal cost.

By afternoon the blue sky had grown dark. Thunder rumbled in the distance.

"Looks like rain again," Peter grumbled.

"It's more to the east, I think," Hunter said.

Heather hoped it wouldn't rain again. She wanted to get the trek over with.

The rain didn't come as they continued, but the sky remained dark. Every now and then lightning could be seen to the east, and the faint sound of thunder.

They came upon the last stream to cross just before Hunter was ready to stop for the night. The banks were higher than the water level, and a makeshift bridge had been thrown across. The water rushed and boiled below the bridge, swollen from the rains. The wind gusted from the east, blowing across the ravine and tossing the spray into the air. Hunter stopped near the bridge and studied the water, looking across to the other side, assessing the possibility of fording at a different location.

"Problem?" Peter asked coming to stand beside Hunter.

"The bank is muddy and slippery from the recent rains. The stream is swollen from the storm to the east and I'm not sure about the safety of the bridge."

"Looks substantial enough," Peter said.

John shook his head. "It looks as if it would wash away with little more rain."

"But it isn't raining here," Peter said. "I'll go first if you want. I'm sure it's safe."

"Hold on a moment," Hunter said. He went to the edge and stepped on the bridge. Bouncing lightly, he stepped out. It was little more than a wide plank laid from bank to bank. The seething water beneath was too deep to try to wade across even if it hadn't been augmented by the recent rain. He remembered Alan's notes about this one last crossing before the lodge. There was no other easy way to cross so if they didn't go this way, they'd have to find another way at perhaps some distance from the trail.

"I say we go," Peter said.

"Up to Hunter," John said.

Hunter looked at Heather, "Your vote?"

"I say it's up to you."

He almost smiled then looked back at the water. "We go. But we take some precautions. Anyone falling into the water would be swept away. John, you have some rope, I do, too. We have a lifeline from person to person."

"Agreed."

In only a few moments, Hunter had tied a length of line around a sturdy tree near the bridge. The wind rose and fell, covering the wet plank with spray.

"John, you cross first. Tie up to one of those trees on the other bank. Peter you'll follow, then Heather, and I'll bring up the rear. The campsite is just a mile or so beyond this stream and we'll stop for our last night."

"Good enough." John tied a length of rope around his waist coiling a length to use on the other side. Then he handed the other end to Peter. "Tie off far enough that I can get across with slack," he said.

Hunter did the same with his rope, tying one end to the tree, the other around his waist. Leaving slack the length of the bridge, he tied the other end around Heather's waist.

"The minute you're across, have John untie you and tie the line to a tree. You wouldn't be heavy enough to hold me if I fall, and I don't want to pull you in. I'll wait before crossing until you two get it secured to a tree, right?"

"Okay. It'll be all right, won't it?" she asked. Heather trusted Hunter completely, but the damp board looked flimsy and insubstantial across the narrow gorge.

"You'll be fine. Just follow as John and Peter go and you'll be across in no time."

Heather tried to listen, but could only feel his hands at her waist, the tingling sensation felt through the layers of clothes, as if he'd touched her bare skin. She looked at him, so close, yet so distant. He hadn't shaved for several days, the beard gave him a rakish air. He looked confident and competent and she knew she trusted him completely.

He tried the knot, then picked up his pack.

"When you're across, tie it to the tree and I'll unwind the rope from this tree. But until then, it'll hold us both if the worst case happens."

She nodded, definitely not looking forward to crossing that rickety bridge. But neither Peter nor John had voiced any protest, she would not be the one to do so.

"It's as safe as it's going to be. We don't have a choice."

She gave him a shaky smile, her eyes drawn to the raging water as it swirled around the boulders below, studied the wet wood that was the bridge. She felt mesmerized by the swirling water, unable to take her eyes away. How cold would it be? How strong a force?

She watched Hunter wind the rope around a large pine and then watched as John tied off one end of his rope. He shouldered his pack, took the slack rope in hand and stepped out on the planks. His step was sure, firm and unhurried. Heather tried to memorize where he stepped so she could follow.

In only a moment he was at the other side. When he secured the line, Peter headed out. Once he was safely across, Hunter untied their rope from the tree.

"You're next," he said to Heather.

She moved to the edge of the bridge. It looked worse than ever, but she couldn't stay here, much as she wanted to. John and Peter had made it with no trouble, she'd be across in less than a minute.

She stepped out. The board was smooth, and a little slippery. Carefully she tried to step where John and Peter had.

Just when she thought she'd make it, two-thirds the way across, the planks lurched and she lost her balance. In an instant she plunged off the plank and into icy, swirling water!

Her shoulder slammed into a submerged rock and the water twisted her around, submerging her, throwing her up into the air. For a split second, the pain overshadowed the shock of icy water. Then the cold took away her breath. Water covered her face, dragged her down, the bite of the rope at her waist dug into her, almost cutting her in two.

She tried to turn over, tried to get her face above the water, but her pack was caught on something below the surface. Struggling, panic flared. She had to get up and catch her breath. She couldn't move, she couldn't breathe! She thrashed around, trying to get out of the icy grasp of the fast-running river. Her shoulder burned, her lungs were bursting.

There was a second when the water wasn't there. She gasped for breath, only to get a mouthful of water as it covered her again. She choked, frantic with fear. Was she going to drown in a raging river she didn't even know the name of, in the wilderness she had no business challenging?

Another second of air, this time she got a lungful. It gave her strength. She'd have to do something soon, or she'd freeze to death, or drown. The water was icy! She twisted sideways, but her pack held her. Kicking, twisting, she tried to get free.

Then strong hands reached her, holding her, lifting her face free of the water. She could feel a tugging on her pack and at last she was free, swept downstream on the water's current, yanked to a stop as the rope dug in. But her face was above the water. She could take in wonderful gulps of air.

"Easy, Heather. You're going to make it, honey. Just hang on. The current's strong, but we'll make the bank. Hang on."

It was Hunter. He was in the water with her, he was holding her arm, his hands firm, strong, soothing. She turned and tried to move towards the bank, her panic abating. She would reach shore! He'd taken her back-pack, so she had more mobility. But her shoulder hurt too much to use her left arm. Kicking in boots and jeans wasn't very productive. She felt virtually helpless, clinging to Hunter, struggling to reach land.

He reached the bank, never letting go of her. It was hard to scramble up the steep and muddy side. They were at least a dozen feet below where the plank bridge had been. Twice Hunter slipped back, but the third time he reached the top. Half dragging her, half helping her, they scrambled away from the icy clutches of the stream and reached solid land.

Heather lay there, gasping for air. Hunter pulled her into his arms, his mouth coming down hard against her cold lips. Eagerly Heather reached up to hold him closer, reveling in the hot feel of his mouth, the delight that coursed through her. Maybe she had died and gone to heaven.

Then reaction set in and she shivered in the cold, despite the warmth where Hunter touched her. He pulled back when he felt her shiver.

"You two okay?" John yelled across from the opposite bank.

"We will be as soon as we get out of these wet clothes and into something dry," Hunter yelled back.

Heather drew in more air, it was wonderful to breathe again.

"Come on, Heather, we're not in the clear yet," he said.

Hunter helped her to her feet, reaching for her backpack.

"I can't believe we aren't dead," she said, shivering with cold. Her shoulder hurt like crazy. But she was alive.

"That's why we had the safety rope. Come on. Your things will be wet, but I took off my pack before jumping in after you, so we'll get some warm clothes from that."

"You jumped in after me?" She could hardly speak for the chattering of her teeth, but the thought shocked her. "You could have been killed."

"So could you have. Did you think I'd take that chance?"

"I guess I thought you'd just pull me up with the rope."

"Impossible against that current. Besides, your pack was caught on one of the rocks."

He'd risked his own life to save her. She was stunned.

"You could have been killed. You didn't have to come into the water after me."

"Yes, I did."

Heather thought through the implications, but she couldn't concentrate.

"I'm so cold," she said, her teeth chattering.

"I know, me, too. We've got to get dry. Warm and dry. Can you help me?"

She was almost too numb to move at all. Her mind was functioning very slowly, everything seemed like a monumental effort. She sat up, her fingers wouldn't work. All she could do was shiver and breathe, still so grateful for air.

"Come on, Heather, you need to get warm. Take off these wet things. I'll get some clothes from my bag." He moved back toward his backpack. She started to follow. Every step was agony, sending shafts of pain into her shoulder.

"Ohhh, I really hurt my shoulder," she said, gritting her teeth in an effort to keep from chattering.

"How badly?" He was instantly attentive.

"Enough that it hurts like crazy."

"I'll check it when you change."

They slowly walked to his pack.

"I'll erect the tent for privacy," he said. John and Peter were on the opposite side, watching them. He called over to explain what they were doing.

She shivered again and wondered if she'd ever feel warm again. Even the pain of her shoulder was beginning to fade as she felt tired and sleepy.

"Come on, you're suffering from hypothermia," he said once the tent was set. He pulled her in behind him and drew in his backpack. In only a moment he yanked out a flannel shirt.

Taking off her jacket and shorts took only a moment. He wrapped her in the flannel, looking at her shoulder as he covered her.

"It's badly bruised. Is it dislocated?" he asked.

She rotated it and winced. "I don't think so, but it really hurts."

She still shivered violently with the cold. The air chilled her through and through.

"Take everything off. I have some jeans you can wear. Too large, but at least they're warm."

"What about you? You're cold as well."

"I'm already changing."

She looked at him, noting the shirt he'd already pulled off. He made short work of shedding his shoes and jeans and pulled on a new pair while she could hardly move. Slowly she forced the wet pants off but was stymied by her hiking boots. Hunter soon dealt with that, taking off them and the cold socks.

In a few moments she was in dry clothes, and bundled in his sleeping bag, shivering still.

Talking to her in his warm voice, calm, authoritative, she kept focus on his words. Her fingers were not responding to her bidding. She felt like all thumbs. She wanted to do as he said, but just couldn't move faster.

"Come on, I'll help." Hunter brought a big towel over and handed it to her. He dried her hair, keeping the rest of her in the sleeping bag.

As she began to gradually warm, every ache and pain throughout her body began to throb—where the rope had tightened, where her hip had grazed a boulder, now her shoulder.

Tears flooded her eyes. She willed them not to fall. She was safe. The water had soaked her, scared her, but she was safe. Thanks to Hunter.

"Let me look at it," he said, gently probing the swelling in her shoulder.

His touch caused agony. She drew in her breath sharply, tears falling despite her efforts. Her shoulder throbbed in time with her pulse, shooting pain at every touch, even with the light covering of the flannel shirt.

He glanced at her and swore under his breath. "I know this hurts, but I've got to see how bad it is. Then I'll check for a phone signal and call for help. Hang on."

His voice was warm, strong. She remembered how he'd talked to her in the river. He was someone she could trust, could lean on. She should have realized that years ago, tried to work something out between them, despite the accident that had changed so much.

But she'd been so afraid—afraid of losing her mother after her father's death; afraid of holding Hunter back when he wanted so desperately to escape the kind of life his father had had. Afraid of her own ability to make it.

CHAPTER EIGHT

HER shoulder was swollen and there was already a dark bruise showing on the side. She twisted to see if she could see behind her.

"It's turning black and blue already," he said, easing the shirt back on her shoulder. "But I don't think it's dislocated."

"It's not. I'll be fine soon. Don't call anyone. I can manage." She stared at him, aware of the cold, the pain, the serious trouble she was in so close to him. She should be worried about the injury, but her only concern was not to leave the trip a moment earlier than she had to. It could be the last time she saw Hunter Braddock.

"We still have to worry about hypothermia. Once you're dry and warm, I'll check it again, okay?"

He made it sound as if it would be all right. She nodded and tried to will herself to become warm.

"Wait a minute and I'll help," he said roughly. He opened the sleeping bag enough to crawl inside, cradling her in his arms.

"My body heat will warm you faster this way," he said. His legs were around hers, his arms held her gently, pressing her into the warmth of his body. He rested his chin on the top of her head, surrounding her with warmth and awareness.

Heather grew warmer faster than she thought possible. One moment she was freezing, the next, so hot she wanted to push back the covers and get some air. Not only was she heating up fast, she was growing more and more aware of Hunter on a physical level. His heart beat strongly under her ear, his arms held her as he had so long ago. She could smell the unique scent of the man she'd loved. That she loved this day. Drawing a deep breath, she savored the scent, memorizing it for the long years ahead when they'd no longer be together.

She had not planned to leave ten years ago, had not made memories she could take out and treasure. She had the happy days as a bittersweet memory of what might have been. Now she knew what lay in the future, but she wanted to store memories for the days ahead.

He ran his fingers through her hair. "It's almost dry," he said, combing through again and again. His touch mesmerized. She closed her eyes, enjoying the exquisite feel of his hand soothing her over and over as he rubbed the shiny strands softly, over and over.

Endless moments seemed to float by. Heather almost fell asleep. Then she shook her head. Time to end this.

"What about the others?"

"They made it across. You warm enough to try again? How is your shoulder?"

"Not much choice, is there?" She asked. "You said we had to cross or retrace several days' worth of hiking."

"If you can get across, I'll have John and Peter build a fire. Keep you warm. We were going to stop soon anyway, might as well camp on the other bank. Then if you can walk out, we'll head for home in the morning."

"I can manage. It's not my feet, it's my shoulder. I don't need Search and Rescue called in."

"Then let's do it."

She slowly left the cocoon of the sleeping bag, shivering in the cool air.

"Your hiking boots are wet," he said.

"I had some tennis shoes in my pack. Oh, they'll be wet, too."

"Everything you have is wet. But some of it can dry tonight. Put on another pair of my socks and then try your boots. Once we're across, you can take them off and put them by the fire to dry."

She eyed the insubstantial bridge. "Always supposing I can make it across this time."

"I've got a better plan. I'll tie a rope to the tree, cross first and tie it to the other side, coming back for you with the rope John used. You'll have two railings to hold on to as you cross. I'll take a backpack across each trip."

"I can manage," she said, feeling totally unable to manage, but not wanting to confess that to Hunter. She had not managed things very well a decade ago. She could understand if he didn't believe she could do any better now.

"This will work. Just get your boots on."

She was only halfway listening, more concerned with how cold she was, and the acute pain of her shoulder.

She closed her eyes, suddenly tired, exhausted. If he said it would work, then she believed him.

In short order he made it across the narrow plank bridge and conferred with the others on the far side. Heather watched dully, wishing her shoulder would ease up a little.

"And while I'm wishing that," she murmured, "I'll wish I was home in my own bed where I'd be warm and cozy."

Despite Heather's fear of crossing the treacherous bridge again, the maneuver went smoothly. In less than a few moments, she joined John and Peter on the far side. They had built a roaring fire and its warmth felt heavenly. She kicked off her damp boots and wiggled her toes toward the flame. She watched as Hunter came across a second time, and left the ropes in place. For the next group to use, he said.

She shuddered, remembering the frantic moment when she knew she was falling, when she hit the water and when she couldn't get any air.

"Lucky we had on the rope." She looked up at him. "Thank you, Hunter, you saved my life."

"It pays to be prepared." Hunter was not prepared for the kick in the stomach her look gave him. Was it an old Chinese proverb that said if you saved someone's life it was yours? For one glorious moment he considered what that would mean to him. He'd claim her. She'd have to return to Denver with him, stay with him forever.

That was a pipe dream if he ever saw one. He turned to the men and discussed making camp where they were. The fire was blazing, it wouldn't take much to prepare the evening meal and everyone could rest up for the last day of the hike.

He was worried about Heather's shoulder.

"She won't be able to carry her backpack, that's for sure," he said.

"I'm right here," she called from beside the fire. "I can carry it on my good shoulder."

"I doubt it," Hunter said.

"We'll divide up your things and each take a portion," John said.

"Or leave it all here and I'll come back for it later," she offered.

"We'll divide the things."

Hunter rigged a line with a short length of rope between two trees and draped the wet clothes over it as close to the fire as he could get them. He shook out her sleeping bag, it was damp, but being so compressed in its bag, it had not absorbed a lot of water. Maybe it would be dry by night. Some of her things were only damp, the waterproofing of the bag had held as long as it could. The fact everything was packed tightly had also precluded the water soaking through. But most things were too damp for comfort. The line soon sagged under the weight of the clothes.

Hunter built the fire bigger, clearing a wide space around it to make sure it didn't spread. Then he came and sat beside Heather.

"How are you doing??" he asked.

"I'm toasty warm and don't want to move." The effort was more than she could make right now. Everything hurt, ached or was cold. She just wanted to sit still and hope she'd feel better soon.

"What do we do now?" she asked.

"Make camp as we discussed. We'll get a good night's rest and see how you feel in the morning. If you are fit enough, we'll hike back to the lodge. If not, John and Peter can hike out and send help."

"I'm walking out on my own," she vowed.

"We'll see how you feel."

"I'm walking!"

He almost laughed at her stubborn stance. Then looked away. There was a lot about Heather he still found appealing. He enjoyed bantering with her. Liked seeing her first thing in the morning.

When he'd held her in the tent across the stream to warm her, it had been all he could do to refrain from kissing her. He'd wanted her as strongly as ever.

He hadn't a clue how Heather felt about the two of them. Did she have regrets or had things evened out for her and she was now content with the way her life had gone?

"Ever have regrets?" he asked.

"All the time," she said promptly.

"About us, I mean."

She hesitated. He suddenly didn't want to hear what she had to say.

"Forget it. I'll see if we can rig a bucket to lower into the water. Be nice to have some coffee with dinner and again in the morning."

He rose and walked away before she could say anything. If she had to think about it, she couldn't have had the regrets he was hoping for. She couldn't still wish they could go back in time and do things differently.

"Darn it!" Heather knew she'd blown her chance to try to make things right. So much for John's assessment that fate had given her a second chance. Every time she thought she had an opening to talk to Hunter, it was gone. Maybe she'd have one more shot tonight in their tent. But after that, she could foresee no chance to talk to Hunter without the others hearing. And giving Peter an earful was not something she wanted to do.

But Hunter gave her no openings in the evening that followed. He was solicitous and caring, but stayed by the fire when she went to their tent. They had to share a sleeping bag, hers was still too damp. Or was he planning to stay awake all night to avoid being that close to her, she wondered when she crawled into the bag alone.

Her shoulder still hurt like crazy. She had to lie on her other side, and even then the throbbing kept her from falling quickly asleep. But she did doze. The next thing she knew, Hunter joined her in the sleeping bag. His warmth was most welcome.

She awoke later, cold and aching. Her shoulder was throbbing, the weight of the sleeping bag adding to her discomfort. She tried to shift positions, but bumped right into Hunter.

He was sleeping. Warm and solid. She eased closer, glad for the warmth. She was tired, but wide-awake. The throbbing didn't ease and she couldn't find a comfortable position. She tried moving to the other side. After a few minutes, she turned over on her back. Nothing.

She was almost in tears with the pain and discomfort. She just wanted to go back to sleep.

A warm hand reached across her waist and drew her closer.

"What's wrong?" His chest was hard, warm, close. She relaxed against him.

"I can't get comfortable," she fretted.

"Shoulder bothering you?"

She nodded, relaxing against his solid strength.

"I can get you some more aspirin, want some?"

"Might help."

It did, but not much.

When Hunter settled back down, he pillowed her head on his arm, his other one pulling her close. She relaxed, feeling safe and warm.

Gradually her awareness of Hunter drove all thought of her aches and pains from her mind. His hand gently rubbed the flannel of her shirt, near her waist. Did he not realize the havoc he was wreaking with her senses? She was impatient with the material separating his hand from her skin. She wanted him to push it aside and caress her directly.

She reached down and took his hand in one of hers, lacing her fingers through his, moving to fit his body more closely.

"What are you doing?"

"Stopping your hand." She barely breathed.

He was silent for a moment, then, "Sorry." But she didn't believe him.

"You are a disturbing person to be around," she murmured softly.

"Go to sleep."

That brought her down quickly.

She was fretful, uncomfortable and anxious to end this time together and get home. Back to the routine, back to her mother and her needs.

She lay awake and thought about her mother. She was sure she'd manage fine at Susan and Saul's. In fact, her mother seemed to manage when Heather wasn't around. But not for long.

Why not? Why hadn't her mother pushed to do more, be more independent? Didn't she want that?

Not according to Susan. Her aunt constantly talked about her mother keeping her tied fast to her apron strings. She urged Heather to break free and have a life, but Heather had always thought her mother needed her too much.

With some distance, she was questioning that assumption.

Worse case, her mother could hire a companion, someone to help her with personal things that were beyond Amelia. But did that have to be Heather?

What if she did leave, moved to another city like Denver? There was other family in Seattle who could help out if Amelia needed it.

Heather allowed herself to fantasize that Hunter wanted to be close to her because he cared for her. She could feel the solid warmth of his body all along hers. The weight of his arm, the warmth of his hand entwined with hers was heavenly. She sighed gently, happy for a few moments. On that note, she fell asleep, a smile on her lips, vague plans for a brighter future in the back of her mind.

When Heather awoke in the morning she was alone in the sleeping bag. She sat up, almost groaning aloud at the pain in her shoulder. Favoring it, she quickly dressed and crawled from the tent. Her boots were right by the opening. They were dry and warm. She put them on and headed for the fire.

"Sleep well?" Hunter asked.

"Yes, thank you. I'm ready to go."

"How's the shoulder?"

"Not bad." It hurt, but so did the rest of her. She hoped she'd be able to put one foot in front of another, but her hope was exercise would loosen the muscles and make the hike easier. They'd reach the lodge before late afternoon, Hunter had said last night.

Of course, she still had the drive back to Seattle, but she could stop at a motel along the way and find a hot shower!

He was studying her.

"What?"

"Just trying to figure how far you'll make it."

"All the way."

He raised an eyebrow. "That'll be a novel experience," he said.

She flushed at his reference. "Hunter, I've apologized. I tried to explain. If you are not going to listen, at least stop making snide remarks."

"You left for my own good," he repeated.

"Yes."

"You had so little confidence in me that you had to make the decision for me?"

"Of course not. That's not the point."

"Of course it is. Heather, you took away my chance to make the decision. You threw away our marriage without even giving me a say in anything. I don't believe it was for my own good, I think it was for your own good. When the chips were down, you went running home to Mom."

"She needed me, Hunter. My father had just died. It was years before we stopped practically living at hospitals and rehab centers."

"I wouldn't know about that, would I? You decided I wasn't man enough to handle it and left—*for my own good.*"

"Not man enough? Hunter are you crazy? Of course you've always been man enough. But you had a hard time coming up with the money for college. We had none. As I told you, we had to sell our house. If my uncle Saul hadn't helped out finally with medical bills and getting me coverage with my mother as a dependent on the company medical plan, I don't know where we would be today. I couldn't expect you to deal with that."

"Why not? You did."

She looked at him. The enormity of her mistake almost knocked her flat. She had denied him the choice. She had robbed them both and had no one to blame but herself.

"It was different for me," she tried to explain. "It was my family. My mother needs me. I have to be there with her."

"And that's the whole point, isn't it, Heather? They were your family, I never was. Just a fling you made legal in college, easily shed when it became inconvenient."

"No, it wasn't like that."

"Then tell me exactly how it was."

Heather looked around as if seeking inspiration. John and Peter were standing near their tent watching her. Had they heard everything? She looked at Hunter. None of her explanation was going the way she wanted.

"It seemed the logical thing at the time," she said flatly. She was not going to continue trying to make him see her side of it with two strangers hanging on every word.

"Love isn't supposed to be logical, it's supposed to be binding. My mother didn't know that and apparently you didn't, either. It sounds to me as if you have blinded yourself to life's realities. You tie yourself to your mother to make your gesture noble and grand, to justify what you've done. But you are not doing her any favors, and you're cheating yourself of life. But it's a great excuse, isn't it? I can't do anything because of my mother. Hold on to that, Heather. It'll be the only comfort you'll have in the years to come." He rose and walked to the edge of the ravine, heading downstream.

John nudged Peter and the two of them walked to the bank of the ravine, giving her a sense of privacy.

Heather wished the earth would open up and swallow her. Hunter was wrong. She wasn't clinging to her mother to justify what she'd done. Her mother needed her. And she did know that love was binding. She had yearned for it all her life, thought she found it with Hunter, and then had made a grand gesture to sacrifice all in the name of love, only to find she was miserable and he was too. All she'd sacrificed was her one chance at happiness.

* * *

Hunter strode along the water's edge, furious at both himself and Heather. How dare she think she knew everything—to take away his choice to make decisions for his own life. Or was it her clever way to put a positive spin on the past so he'd consider Jackson and Prince for the contract?

He didn't know the woman at all. What they'd once had ended years ago. They'd both been young and so caught up in hormones they couldn't think rationally, at least that's what he remembered about their time together.

He'd moved on and obviously Heather had as well—at least in the direction she wanted. If she wished to be a caregiver to her mother all her life, so be it.

He had never found another woman to love completely because of her. Maybe this trip would open his eyes at last and free him from the past.

His temper eased as he walked. Soon he stopped and studied the roiling water for a long moment. He had to get this group back to the lodge and bid them farewell. Then he'd return to Denver and let Alan know in no uncertain terms it had been a dumb idea from start to finish to try camping with ad executives.

Peter drove him crazy. He liked John, but the man rarely pushed his own company's ideas. As for Heather—he'd tried to envision dealing with her in a business setting for the next ten years or so. He'd failed.

He could only think about her eyes, and the sadness they held. Or her laughter which warmed his soul. How could they deal together as mere acquaintances when they'd once meant so much to each other?

No answers appeared and after a few more moments,

he turned and resolutely headed back to camp. When he arrived, John and Peter were sitting next to Heather. The tents had been folded and put away, the backpacks stacked nearby.

The fire was dwindling. It wouldn't take much to ensure it was out before they left.

"Ready to leave?" Hunter asked.

"As we'll ever be," John said rising slowly. "We divided Heather's things among the three of us."

"Good thinking."

"I still think I could manage," she said, rising.

But by the way she held her arm against her body, Hunter had his doubts she'd last the day, much less be able to carry a backpack on one shoulder.

"We'll handle it. Let's head out." He donned his pack—it felt only a little heavier than before—and picked up Heather's empty one. He led off, Peter falling into step.

"I didn't realize you and Heather had been married," the man said.

Hunter didn't care to discuss the past—especially with a near stranger like Peter.

"What we had ended ten years ago."

"So it won't influence the outcome of the selection process?"

"Not in any way that will impact you," Hunter said shortly. He lengthened his stride slightly. The sooner they reached the lodge, the sooner he could leave them all behind and return to Denver.

Peter became quiet, a blessing Hunter didn't question. If the man could keep quiet, maybe he could fall into the rhythm he usually found hiking, enjoying the beauty of nature and the expending of energy of his muscles moving in easy harmony. The trail was not steep, nor particularly difficult. Listening to the sounds of the forest was soothing. He glanced back to see how Heather was doing, frowning when he saw her beside John.

Heather was at a loss of what she could say to Hunter to make things better between them. Each moment took them closer to parting, and things had not improved. If she'd been given a second chance, she'd blown it. Between that thought and her shoulder, it was a miserable hike. Each step she took jarred her shoulder. She had difficulty walking. What she really wanted to do was sit down and not move for a day or two until her shoulder felt better.

She also wanted Hunter to understand her side of things. To forgive her for ending their marriage and say he'd like to spend time with her.

The way he was charging ahead, she'd be lucky to say goodbye at the end of the hike. He'd probably jump into his car and tear out of the parking lot.

The pain in her shoulder didn't bother her as much as the pain in her heart. She'd tried so long and hard to get over Hunter. Caring for her mother, she devoted herself to her needs. She'd convinced herself a few years back that she was ready to move on, that one day she'd find a man who would love her as much as Hunter had, and whom she could love in return, as long as he could also deal with her mother.

Was Hunter right? Was she hiding behind her mother's needs as a way to retreat from the world?

Her first look at Hunter a few days ago and she knew she'd been fooling herself that she'd ever find someone else. She loved him. Had from the moment she met him and she suspected she'd love him forever. No other man would do. She'd spend her days alone rather than settle for second best.

And if she didn't make some changes in her life, that's exactly what would happen in her future, she'd be alone.

Yet her mother did depend upon her. What could she do?

When she stumbled a second time in less than five minutes, John reached out his hand and caught her good arm.

"Let's sit and rest. You're pushing it too much." He called to the others and guided Heather to a fallen log.

She sat gratefully, her shoulder throbbing in rhythm with her heartbeat.

"Heather needs to rest," John said when Hunter and Peter retraced their steps to join them.

She met Hunter's eyes, hoping he could read the apology she tried to voice.

He hunkered down beside her and looked at her with concern.

"How's the shoulder?"

"Bothering me a bit."

He reached out and gently rubbed it.

Heather was mesmerized. His touch was so gentle, his eyes dark and warm. She thought she could lose herself in the velvety softness. Her expression must have given her away because she saw his jaw tighten when he clenched his teeth. He looked away. She let go of her breath, not realizing she had been holding it. She could feel her heart beating heavily in her chest. She didn't look away, feasting her eyes on him. Longing to reach out for him and have him reach out for her. Longing to tell him she would always be there for him. If he wanted her. Circumstances had changed. Could he ever find it in him to give her a second chance? To give them another chance?

"We can make a cold compress at the next creek," he said standing. "If the swelling goes down, it'll be less uncomfortable."

"No, I don't want to slow us down. I'm fine."

John shook his head.

Heather frowned. "Okay, maybe not perfectly fine, but capable of moving on. Let's finish this hike today."

The hours passed slowly as Heather needed more and more frequent rest stops. She hated being the cause of everyone hanging around, but didn't know what to do except soldier on. She didn't want to spend another night with Hunter in the close proximity they'd shared—not with things so wrong between them.

Peter and John built a fire when they stopped for lunch. Hunter started coffee, and divided up the food. "I'm not exactly sure how far it is, but I'd say we'll easily make it before dark."

"I'm all for that," Heather said, ambling around the small clearing, hoping to keep herself limber. Her shoulder she could almost ignore. She felt stiff all over, however, and longed for the end of the trek.

Hunter rose to get the rest of the lunch, and walked beside her. He leaned over and said softly, "I was right, you look good in my jeans." He rested his hand briefly on her hip, the jeans stretched taut over her smooth skin. Heather felt almost as if he'd branded her, the heat from his hand went straight through her. Her heart tripped faster and butterflies began dizzying cancans in her stomach.

She was trembling as she swung away. She had to get ahold of herself, she couldn't let his every touch inflame her or she'd become a blithering idiot. She didn't think he was softening. If she told him how she truly felt, he'd likely accuse her of trying to get the account. Or coming on to him because he had more money now than ten years ago. She would be unbearably hurt if he ever thought that.

By the time the lunch was finished, she felt ready to tackle the remaining trail home. She had to, she didn't want to extend this bittersweet time. She wanted to go home, sort things out and decide exactly what she wanted in her future.

Besides Hunter, that was.

Progress in the afternoon was slow, but steady. Heather neither fell, nor held back. At the end of an hour, however, she was ready for a rest.

Hunter handed her the canteen and she drank greedily. The water felt so cool and refreshing going down.

"How're you doing?" he asked, squatting beside her. He kept his pack on, only laying hers down. It would be a brief rest stop.

"I'm hanging in there." She smiled, happy to be resting; glad, despite everything, to be in his company. Wishing she could rest her head against his shoulder, feel his arm around her, she gripped the canteen and tried not to burst into tears.

"You're doing good, Heather. Better than I expected. Keep it up and we'll be back to the lodge in no time."

She nodded, warmed by his praise, ignoring the discomfort she felt. They had not come very far in an hour. She resolved to make it to the end no matter what.

"I'm ready." She wasn't, but couldn't stay all day resting from the short distance they had traveled since lunch.

Just after three o'clock they came into the clearing where the lodge was located, only yards from their vehicles.

"We made it!" Heather said in surprise.

"Good job," Hunter said.

In no time the men had put her things in the trunk of her car. John was the first to leave, shaking hands with the others, urging Hunter to plan on another trip, without the awarding of a contract as a motive.

Peter made one last push for his agency, then left.

Hunter walked Heather to her car.

"You going to make it home all right?" he asked.

"Yes." She wasn't sure if she would make it tonight, but she'd leave with her head held high.

"Goodbye, Heather."

"Wait, Hunter. What about—"

"Alan will announce the ad agency we select, probably early next week."

"That wasn't what I was concerned about. What about us?"

"There is no us, Heather."

But as if to put a lie to his words, he drew her into his arms and kissed her.

His lips were warm. His touch was electrifying as he drew her against him, and his kiss deepened, lengthened. She was lost. Her hands pressed to his chest, her hips drawn tight against his. She couldn't move, and had no desire to do so, unless to get closer. His tongue probed for a response that she was only too glad to give. She rubbed against him almost like a kitten, seeking closer contact. Her hand threaded itself in the soft thickness of his hair, her body cried out for more. She never wanted to let go.

His touch soothed and excited, massaged and caressed. Heather grew warm and soft and relaxed. She savored the sensual pleasure at the feel of his hands against hers, his skin touching hers.

Slowly he ended the caress, drawing back, taking her hand from his neck. He steadied her long enough for her to regain her balance.

"You're dangerous," he said softly, his hand softly caressing her neck as if reluctant to lose touch.

"I don't want to say goodbye," she said.

"Then let's just say see you around," he said, stepping back. "Have a nice life, Heather."

"I love you, Hunter," she blurted out. "I always have. I'm so sorry I left before. Please, can't we try again? I don't want to say goodbye."

Without another word, he shook his head, turned and crossed to his vehicle, putting the backpack in, ignoring the woman standing beside her car.

Heather swallowed hard. She'd said it, and it hadn't

mattered. Slowly she got into her car, started the engine and backed from the parking space.

With a quick glance in her rearview mirror at the man who hadn't turned around, she headed toward Seattle.

CHAPTER NINE

HUNTER turned as her car left the lot, watching it as it reached the road and turned west.

I love you, she'd said. *Can't we try again?*

For what—another few weeks together until her family needed her and then he lost her again? He wasn't strong enough for that. He didn't want to be drawn to her, didn't want to hope there'd be something that would eventually make everything come out right. Truth to tell, he resented her, that she could make him feel this way after all the years between, make him want her and to hell with the consequences. She'd made her bed, so be it. She'd chosen her mother ten years ago and hadn't looked back. At any time in the ten years she could have called him. She never had.

He looked around the forest, wishing the entire trip had never happened. Then he climbed into the rented SUV and started out. He'd be in Denver tomorrow. Forget about the trip and move on.

By the time she'd driven an hour, Heather was exhausted. Nothing had gone the way she wanted. Why should the trip home be any different? She spotted a motel ahead on the right and turned in when she reached it. She'd get a room, have a hot shower and sleep in a comfortable bed until morning. Things were bound to look better by then.

Tired and miserable, tears welled up in her eyes and slowly spilled over. She didn't want to return home. Not alone. Not to face more lonely years like the last ten had been. She'd given her best shot, told Hunter she loved him, and it hadn't been good enough. What would she do now?

Heather checked into the motel, pleased to find a small coffee shop immediately adjacent. She went to get some hot food, hoping she could stay awake long enough to eat, get to her room and take a hot shower before crashing in bed. She was so tired and disheartened.

Eating energized her. The shower was heavenly. Clean and warm, she crawled into bed to watch television until she fell asleep. It was wonderful to be in a soft bed, instead of the hard ground. Just as she was ready to switch off the light later that evening, she thought of her mother. Everyone expected her back in Seattle tonight. Her mother would be frantic with worry if she didn't show up.

With a sigh, she reached for the phone and dialed her uncle's number.

"Hello?" Susan answered.

"Hi, Aunt Susan, it's me, Heather."

"Hi, honey. Are you home now?"

"No. I'm still in the mountains. I'm staying the night here before driving back. We didn't get to the cars until late." She didn't plan to explain about her shoulder just yet. No need to worry anyone.

"How did Mom do?" she asked.

"She did fine, though I thought she'd never stop complaining. Does she do that at home or are we just the lucky ones?" Susan asked lightly.

Heather instantly grew defensive on behalf of her mother. Yet when she considered it for a moment, she realized her mother did complain a lot.

"I guess that's just her way."

Had she hidden behind her mother's needs as Hunter had said? She'd been away from her for a week now, and realized she didn't want to return home!

"She stopped after I told her to consider all her blessings. There are lots of people worse off than your mother, and without a devoted daughter to watch them. I know she'll be delighted to return home and get away from me."

Suddenly Heather felt as if things were closing in on her. She didn't want to go back to the apartment, didn't want to be confined to work she really didn't like and caring for her mother. She was only twenty-nine, too young to be set in her ways. Too young to have to give up everything to take care of a woman who probably could manage with a minimum of help. For the first time she examined her life and found it wanting.

"Heather?"

"Sorry, I was just thinking," she replied.

"Did you have a good time?"

"Yes and no. I—" Heather closed her mouth. She couldn't tell anyone about running into Hunter. No one in her family knew of her marriage. Except Saul.

"Is Uncle Saul there?"

"He's already gone to bed, want me to wake him?"

"No, no, don't do that. I'll talk to him when I get home." She wished she could to talk to someone. But would Saul lend a sympathetic ear? If anyone would, it would be her aunt.

"I ran into Hunter Braddock on the trip."

"Oh, an old friend?"

"You might say that." Heather leaned back against the pillows on her bed. "He was my husband ten years ago."

Susan's shocked gasp could be clearly heard. "What are you talking about?"

"We were married in college. But I left when Dad died and Mom was so badly injured. He was on the hike. Didn't Saul tell you about Hunter? Apparently he's known all along. He was helpful in ending my marriage, though I only found out about that on this trip."

"Good grief. I had no idea. You say Saul knew? He never even gave me a hint."

"I never told anyone. Once I knew how badly Mom was hurt, I knew I couldn't expect Hunter to take on that burden. So I filed for divorce. But on the trip Hunter said he came to Seattle to see me and Saul sent him packing. No wonder it was so easy to get a divorce." No wonder he never tried to contact her over the years. She'd walked out and her family drove the point home.

"Honey, I never suspected. You poor thing, the burden of losing your dad and then your husband. Well, all I can say is he's not worth a single thought if he couldn't stand by you in your time of need."

Heather blinked, not expecting the condemnation.

"It wasn't his fault, it was mine. And maybe Saul's."

"How do you figure? You didn't cause the accident. I'd say he's a poor excuse of a man to end the marriage because things didn't go perfectly."

"No, I'm not explaining this correctly." Heather quickly told her aunt the story of their dating, of her parents not wanting to even hear about the man who meant so much to her over the Christmas break, and of their brief marriage.

"Oh, Heather," Susan said at the end. "You never even gave him a chance to be with you. Honey, that was cruel."

"I couldn't burden him with my mother and her care. You know it took every cent we had and then some. How fair would that have been to him to saddle him with debts before he was even out of college? He struggled so hard to make it to the university, he deserved more than be saddled with our problems."

"And so you gave him his freedom."

Heather nodded. Then realized her aunt couldn't see her.

"I thought I had. But he doesn't see it that way. He's still furious with me about it. I didn't expect his anger to last so long. I never wanted him angry with me."

"Come on home, honey, and we'll talk. If he's still angry, some strong feelings must still be there. Do you love him?"

Heather burst into tears. "So much I hurt!" she said.

"Come straight here in the morning. We'll sort through everything," Susan said soothingly. "I'll let your mother know to expect you tomorrow. You don't need to talk to her tonight."

Heather hung up, still crying. She thought she'd spent the tears years ago, but saying goodbye a second time had been harder. She loved Hunter, why couldn't they be together forever? What karma kept them apart when that was all she wanted? She couldn't see a way to change things, and it was all her fault. That hurt. Instead of finding rest in sleep, she cried bitter tears far into the night.

Hunter reached Seattle before ten that night. He registered at one of the bigger hotels near downtown and hit the shower. He'd visit the new store in the morning. A spot check never hurt. He was scheduled to return to Denver on an afternoon flight. He wasn't certain he'd keep to that schedule.

Maybe he'd visit the various offices of the agencies vying for his business—starting with Jackson and Prince.

"You're a masochist," he told himself as he stood beneath the hot shower. He didn't need to see Heather again. It had been a hard week. Made even harder by her parting words.

He refused to go down that path again. They'd tried marriage, she'd bolted at the first opportunity, their first hurdle.

What would it be like to be part of her family? To know she'd come no matter what, and give up everything to rally round?

He wished she'd felt that way about him.

What was it about him that women couldn't stay the course? His mother had left. Heather had left. Not that two women made a pattern, but their leaving left a hurt that he didn't care to risk again.

He dried off and walked to the wide window of his room which overlooked downtown Seattle. The lights were sparkling in the darkness. It looked like a fairyland of enchantment. Hunter almost groaned at his fanciful thoughts. Fairyland, indeed. There were men and women working long hours to achieve their goals. He'd made a success of Trails West through the same long hours. He had everything he wanted now. Wishing for something long gone wasn't going to change anything.

He was a success like his father had never been. One day he'd think about marrying again. He'd like a son or daughter to leave the business to.

He stared at the view for endless moments.

For the first time in years Hunter admitted the truth. He wanted what he hadn't had—a family to share his life. Friends were fine; business associates necessary. But nothing touched the deep-down loneliness that surfaced in the night. He achieved what he wanted in business. Time to treat his personal life the same—establish a goal and go for it.

He thought about the women he'd dated over the years. He'd almost asked Janet to marry him. Why hadn't he? She'd have made the perfect wife. She was polished, entertaining and beautiful. Or Brittany. She'd loved the outdoors as much as he did.

But they weren't Heather, something inside whispered.

His father had never gotten over his mother's defection. Was he destined to repeat the pattern, forever yearning for something out of reach?

* * *

Heather arrived in Seattle by eleven the next morning. She had called ahead for an appointment with her doctor to check her shoulder. Reassured with his assessment, and loaded with powerful painkillers, she reluctantly headed for her uncle's home. She regretted telling Susan so much last night. She'd kept the secret for years, why let a low spot in her life change that?

She wanted to talk to her uncle and see what he had to say. Had he not interfered, would Hunter have sought her out and made some overture? Joined her after his final exams like he tried? She wished she could change the past, but that was impossible.

Still, she was glad someone else knew. If nothing else, Aunt Susan would be a confidante to talk to in the future. She was a wise woman.

Wise enough to see Heather was forfeiting her own life in order to cater to her mother. Hiding behind her mother, Hunter had said.

The thought had been growing ever since she left Seattle last week. Maybe it was time to cut the apron strings and let her mother find her own way. She was wheelchair bound, but not incapable of looking after herself. She cooked infrequently, when the mood struck her, but she could prepare her own meals. She had her quilting to occupy her time. And she could have all her old friends around her again if she'd make the effort.

Armed with a new resolution, Heather parked in front of the spacious home of her aunt and uncle. She gave a brief thought for the modest house her parents had owned before medical bills had necessitated its sale. Not as grand as Saul's, it had nonetheless been home as long as Heather remembered. She knew her mother missed the house. In the normal course of events, Heather would have married by now, started a family and found her own place, whether a house or an apartment, it wouldn't matter. As long as she and her husband had love, any place would be home.

Try as she might, the only picture that came to mind was the small student apartment she and Hunter had shared. It had seemed like a palace with him there.

"Hello, Heather." Aunt Susan called from the open doorway, a wide smile of welcome on her face.

Heather got out of her car and walked slowly up the walkway. Butterflies danced in her stomach, but she was determined to make some changes. Her shoulder ached a little, but the medication the doctor had given her was already taking effect. She wished she'd had something like it on the hike. Or that it worked for broken hearts as well as it helped with bruised shoulders.

"Hi, Aunt Susan." She was enveloped in a warm hug, wincing slightly with the pressure on her shoulder.

"What's wrong?"

"I fell while hiking and banged up my shoulder. I've already seen my doctor, and he said I'll be fine in a couple of weeks. But it's sore."

"I thought Saul said it would be a nice camping trip, no danger."

"There was little danger, but we ended up losing two of the men who started due to illness and an accident, and I came limping into the finish, so to speak."

"Come in and tell us all about it. Your mother is anxious to see you."

"And to get home," Amelia said from behind her. She sat in her chair, a frown on her face. "I thought you were coming back yesterday, Heather. I'm more than ready to go home."

"Mother!" Heather was shocked at the overt rudeness. She never would have been permitted to get away with something like. "I'm sure you want to get home, but after all Susan and Saul have done, I think a bit of gratitude wouldn't be out of the question."

Her mother glowered at Susan.

"Can you stay for lunch?" Susan asked.

"Yes," Heather said at the same time her mother said, "No!"

Heather looked at her mother. "You can go along, then, but since Aunt Susan invited me for lunch, I'm staying."

"Heather, how dare you speak to me that way," Amelia said.

"Actually we're in for a long talk, Mom. I'll wait until we're back at the apartment, but things are going to change. Aunt Susan might as well know from the get-go. I'm going to find someone to help you and then I'm moving out."

"Heather!" Amelia looked shocked.

Susan looked surprised, then turned away to hide a smile.

The phone rang and Susan went to answer it.

"What is the matter with you, Heather?" Amelia asked. "It is too much to ask that I go home? I've been in that woman's house long enough."

"I would think you'd be happy Aunt Susan and Uncle Saul let you stay here with them while I was gone. You could have stayed home."

"You know that's not possible."

"Actually, Mom, I think it is definitely possible. And we have to find out exactly how to manage that, because I'm not staying." The idea had grown as she drove in to Seattle, and waited in the doctor's office. Once she was sure her mother could manage, she planned to visit Denver. Maybe if she showed Hunter she would go to him he'd listen.

"I need you," Amelia said. "What happened on this trip to change you?"

"I'm twenty-nine-years old. I want a life besides going to the ad agency and spending all my nights at home with my mother. I love you, you know that. But it's not right to forfeit my life when with a few arrangements you can live as you wish—and I can live as I wish. Did you ever wonder what I wanted?" Heather asked.

"I know I've been a burden," Amelia began, fidgeted with her lap robe. "But when your father died, I had no one else besides you. I can't manage on my own, you know that."

"Mom, you've never been a burden. But you had lots of friends, whom you've turned away over the years. You had interests and activities that got you out of the house. There are many people in wheelchairs who lead perfectly wonderful lives. You can, too."

Amelia stared at Heather like she'd grown a second head.

"I don't know what's come over you," she said.

"I suspect it has to do with one Hunter Braddock," Susan said, joining them in the foyer. "Let's go into the kitchen. I'll prepare lunch while we talk. That was Saul on the phone," she said, leading the way into the back of the house. "He wanted to know exactly what the relationship is between Hunter and Heather these days."

"Who is Hunter Braddock?" Amelia asked, propelling her chair along to keep up with Susan's brisk walk.

"The head of Trails West, the account Saul sent Heather out to get. Apparently the man showed up at Jackson and Prince first thing this morning with interrogation on his mind," Susan said.

Heather followed, bemused. Hunter had gone to the agency? She wished she'd made the effort to go into work. No, on second thought, it would be better if she didn't see him again so soon. She'd made enough of an idiot of herself by practically throwing herself into his arms and exclaiming she loved him. He hadn't wanted to hear that. The thought pricked, but she took a deep breath, willing the ache away. She couldn't dwell on his rejection. She had to hope he'd see things differently when she went to Denver.

"Why in the world would he have done that? What kind of man is he?" Amelia asked, coming to a halt in the center of the large kitchen.

Susan began to pull things from the refrigerator for lunch.

"Actually Saul was curious as to what Mr. Braddock had to say." She glanced at Heather. "And fascinated to see some lingering interest in a relationship between our Heather and Hunter Braddock that goes back some years."

"What relationship?" Amelia asked sharply, looking at Susan then at Heather.

Heather looked at her aunt. "You didn't talk to Uncle Saul?"

Susan shook her head. "I told you, he was already asleep last night. And he left before I awoke this morning. To say he was stunned might be an understatement."

"Tell him what?" Amelia asked.

Heather took a deep breath and faced her mother. "Hunter Braddock was my husband."

"Nonsense. You've never been married."

"Actually I was, Mom. When I was in college. I ended it when I had to come home."

Amelia stared at her. Suddenly her face became stricken.

"You left your husband to come home to care for me?"

Heather nodded. "It wasn't fair to saddle him with all the expenses and all the uncertainty we had facing us. He had so little as a child and worked so hard to get as far as he had in college, I couldn't take that away from him. I know he would have gladly left school to work two jobs to help us out. I couldn't stand for that to happen." She shrugged. It sounded like she hadn't cared, when it really had changed her entire life.

Amelia didn't say a word, she just stared at Heather.

"Any chance he'd want to take up again?" Susan asked. She placed the sandwiches on the plates, dished up a scoop of fruit salad and set the plates round the big kitchen table.

Heather shook her head. "It was weird seeing him after all these years. He's accomplished so much of what he wanted. I was happy to learn that. He's successful, established. I think I did the right thing." She blinked back tears. Doing the right thing had not been easy. And it never stopped hurting.

"The boy you tried to tell us about that Christmas," Amelia said at last. "Your father and I thought it mere infatuation."

"No, Mom. It wasn't. I loved him so much back then I thought I'd die being away from him over Christmas break. I was so disappointed neither you nor Dad would take me seriously. He was important to me, and you dismissed him as nothing. Does a person have to be a magic age before she's allowed to fall in love?"

Amelia looked away. "We thought it would pass. We so wanted you to get a college education. Neither of us had one and we so wanted that for you."

"I wanted it, too. I wanted to be a schoolteacher. I love children. But fate stepped in with the car crash."

"And now here we all are," Susan said. She indicated the food on the table. "It's not too late to go back to college, Heather. I'm sure Saul would let you arrange your hours to attend classes. And Amelia could get a job to help with finances."

"What? I can't—" Amelia trailed off at the glint in Susan's eye.

She turned to Heather. "I didn't know you had married the man. You never told us."

"I wanted to finish the school year with high grades so I could tell you and Dad that being married didn't mean I couldn't graduate. Only, I never even took the final exams."

She sat at the table, barely noticing the ache in her shoulder. Staring at the plates, she tried to work up an appetite. "Thanks for lunch, Aunt Susan."

Susan looked at Amelia. "I love Saul, Amelia. I know you loved Sam. You were devastated when he died, as we all were. Imagine if you had given him up and walked away ten years ago for your family's sake. Heather was young, but I believe she loved that young man. She loves him still. I know I'll love Saul all my life. She's given up a lot for you, the least you can do is make an effort to let her find what she wants from life. Let her go, Amelia. There are other ways for you to manage."

"Heather's all I have," Amelia said softly.

"Mom, that's not true. You have Saul and Susan, the entire Owens clan, the Peterses and your friends from before, if you'd just make an effort to resume the friendships."

"Who wants an old cripple around them?" Amelia asked bitterly.

"Not with your current attitude. But you used to be a lot of fun," Susan said bluntly.

"I think Heather and I need to discuss this further," Amelia said.

"I think so, too, Mom. As soon as we finish lunch, we'll head for home."

"Tell me about the hiking trip," Susan said.

"I don't think we got the account. There was one man there who had an answer for everything. He drove me crazy, but was always hanging around Hunter, so my guess is he has the inside track."

"I'm not at all interested in business," Susan said. "I

want the details about Hunter Braddock and what it was like seeing him ten years later."

Heather smiled sadly. "It was amazing. Hard, wonderful, sad." She could tell them a little about the trip, but not the kisses, not the nights spend fantasizing about what might have been. Not her declaration at their parting. Some things were too private to share.

CHAPTER TEN

HEATHER had no expectations that the discussion with her mother would be easy. Amelia held her peace until they reached their apartment, then began on the complaints about staying with Saul and Susan, how she really needed Heather to help her with her daily routine, and how difficult it would be for her to blend in with mainstream activities. She was sorry to be a burden to her daughter, but she needed Heather. She couldn't possibly manage on her own, no matter what Susan said.

Heather let her run on until she wound down. They were in the living room with Heather on the sofa. Her shoulder hurt. She wanted to go lie down, but this needed to be dealt with first. She still felt as strongly about moving on as she had yesterday. She knew it would be hard, but if she didn't make the move soon, she'd never go.

Her mother had needed her and would always depend on her if she didn't make a push to have her stand on her own. Had she hidden behind her injuries as a way to justify her walking out on Hunter? She hated to think that, but she was beginning to believe it was true. Did that make her feel heroic, sacrificing her own happiness for the good of her mother? Or only human, to make the loss easier to bear?

"Mom, I'm going to be thirty on my next birthday. You had a happy marriage and a daughter when you turned thirty. Don't you want the same for me? Wouldn't you like to be a grandmother? If I don't make some changes, I'll be working for Uncle Saul when I'm eighty, and an old maid to boot."

Amelia frowned. "So are you planning to take up with that Hunter Braddock again? Move to Denver and leave me here all alone?"

"He's moved on, Mom," Heather said sadly. "And I would never leave you all alone. We'll see what we can do to have you manage on your own. Maybe a part-time housekeeper or something."

"And where would we get the money?"

"We'd manage. You could sell some of your quilts. They're quite lovely."

"It's a hobby—"

The knock on the door was unexpected. Heather rose and went to open it, startled to see Hunter standing there.

She looked up into his dear face. She'd thought she wouldn't see him again unless she went to Denver. He stared back at her for a long moment and then reached out to draw her into his arms. He hugged her carefully, considering her shoulder, his mouth lowering to hers, his lips teasing hers. Lightly he kissed her, moving his mouth to the corner of her mouth, capturing her lower lip and softly sucking on it, moving to kiss her again, her soft cheeks, to her throat, back to her hot waiting lips.

Heather forgot everything. She lost track of time and place and her mother. She could only feel the warmth of his lips, the wondrous feeling that spread through her body at his touch. The joy and love that blossomed in his arms.

She tried to capture his lips, she yearned to have him kiss her long and hard, but he wouldn't satisfy her. His kisses teased and tormented, but did not fulfill. His lips were hot and exciting, but they only tantalized, offering only a hope of more. His mouth moved against hers, but would not stop there. He kissed her cheeks, her throat, the line of her jaw.

He was driving her crazy. She held on tightly drowning in the pleasure he evoked. Stars swirled behind her closed lids, though it was only late afternoon. Her breathing became difficult, as she floated on the spiraling sensations his lips brought. She wanted the moment to last forever, never to have to surface to reality. It was magical, and she wanted it to go on for ever. She had thought she'd never see him again, and yet here he was.

He lifted his face, his eyes flashing, his breathing ragged. She stared back at him, her whole being longing for him. His voice was husky when he spoke.

"Do you bewitch all men you see? Do you entice them with your innocent brown eyes, your soft skin and trusting manner? You'd tempt a saint, and we all know I'm not even close to a saint. I wanted to stay away, but couldn't. Your uncle told me where you lived."

"I didn't think I'd see you again," she said, tracing the outline of his lips with her finger. He took it in his mouth, laving the tip with his tongue, holding it gently with his lips. She felt the shock to her toes.

She moved her finger, to place her lips there. He responded and she was in heaven again. Her fingers threaded themselves through the thickness of his hair, reveling in the tactile sense she experienced with him. His scent was of trees and open spaces, his body hard and exciting.

"What are you doing here?" she asked.

"I came to see you, of course." He kissed her again.

Was it just another chance to say goodbye? Was his flight to Denver leaving soon?

His mouth closed over hers and she was lost to his embrace as his mouth drank deeply from the depth of her love. His kiss plunged the depth of her being. His hands traced her body, skimming along her back, ever conscious of her injured shoulder. Every nerve ending quivered with longing.

Long minutes later he drew back, gazing down into her eyes, his own dark and sad.

"Where do we go from here, Heather?"

"Heather?"

She turned and looked over her shoulder at her mother. Sighing softly, she released herself from his arms. "Hunter, come and meet my mother."

"Mrs. Jackson," he said, stepping into the apartment. He seemed to dwarf the room, Heather thought when the door closed behind them. He shook hands with her mother and then went to sit on the sofa at Amelia's invitation.

"So you're the man who left my daughter when she needed him most," she said.

"Mother! That's so wrong. Don't even go there. I left Hunter. He didn't fully know our situation. Only that I wanted out of the marriage. When he came to try to talk to me, Saul sent him away. Hunter did absolutely nothing wrong."

Hunter looked surprised at Heather's defense. Sitting on the sofa he studied Amelia Jackson.

"At the time, I thought Heather had come into some money with the death of her father and didn't want to be bothered to stay married," he said easily. "Wasn't that the impression you wanted to give?" he asked Heather.

She nodded miserably. "I'm so sorry. But I stand by what I did."

"Seems we both have to stand by what you did," he commented.

"What brings you here today?" Amelia asked.

"Something Heather said to me recently," he said, his eyes only for Heather.

"What?" she asked, hope blossoming. From the kiss at the door, he wasn't immune to her. Was it only physical? Or was there something more?

"And that was?" Amelia asked, annoyed the attention of the other two people in the room seemed to be elsewhere.

"She said she loved me, I came to see if it is true."

"Yes," Heather said, hope blossoming. Did it mean he was interested?

"I'm not giving the account to Jackson and Prince," he said.

"I don't care. I mean, I do care, it would be a good match. But that's not why I told you. Is that what you thought?"

"Where do you want to go from here?" he asked.

"Wherever you want."

"Dating occasionally?"

Heather swallowed. She wanted more, but if that's all he had to give, she'd take it. She nodded.

"Will you come to Denver?"

She nodded again. She'd planned that. He had to know she'd do anything for him.

"Heather," Amelia said in panic.

"Mother, this is really between me and Hunter."

His eyes lightened in amusement. They never left hers. "Will you marry me again?"

Heather thought her heart would stop. She flung herself into his arms and held on for dear life. "Yes I would in a heartbeat! I love you, Hunter, I have from that first day in the student union when we met."

He almost crushed her in his embrace, his mouth finding hers, igniting the flame that had burned between them. She held him tightly, clung to him, happiness growing. Was it true? Did he really want her to marry him?

She pulled back. "It's not for the money, you know that, don't you?"

"What money?"

"Your money. I make enough to support my mother and me, I don't need your money."

He laughed at that, hugging her closer. "I never thought you were after me for my money, but I have enough to provide for you and your mother. On the condition you marry me again and never leave. We'll start up where we left off. Only be warned, if any other family emergency crops up, I won't let you go. I learned my lesson last time. We're in this together or not at all!"

"I wouldn't leave you again, Hunter. Give me the rest of your life to prove it to you. We'll be so happy. I love you so much! I'm glad I told you in the parking lot."

"That helped. But it was seeing you almost killed when you fell into the water that made me realize no matter what had happened to us in the past, nothing could change if we didn't change it ourselves. You could have been killed. Foolish pride has no place when something as important as love between us was concerned. Your declaration had me thinking all the way to Seattle. My mind was made up even before I went to see your uncle. You are mine. I want to be with you, to be your husband again."

Heather felt the warmth in her heart spread as she snuggled against the man she loved. He loved her, still wanted her to share his life with him as he had so many years ago.

"Why did you go to see Saul?" she asked.

"To tell him I was going to ask you to marry me again. And to discuss the business climate of Seattle. I'm not taking any chances this time, I'm going to move my part of the corporate office here. I've already been in touch with Trevor."

"You'd move to Seattle?" Heather looked at him in amazement.

"Why not? With the expansion of Trails West into the Pacific Northwest, it'll pay to have one of the owners close at hand. And you and I can enjoy the amenities offered—like hiking when we want. We can ski at Ranier, or hop up to B.C. I'll enjoy the climate here as well as Denver. Maybe better."

"But that's not the real reason," she said.

"No, the real reason is you and your mother."

"You were right, I was trying to justify my actions by making her the focal point of my life," Heather confessed. "If I had to be here for her, I could live with knowing I threw away my chance at happiness. I couldn't stand what I had done if it had been for nothing."

"She's your mother. I realize I would do the same for my dad. Family is important, Heather. But you and I are also family. I want us to be family forever."

"You don't trust me, do you?" she asked, sitting up.

"What are you talking about?"

"You think if you live here in Seattle, I can't leave you again if something bad happens."

"There is that."

"But I would never leave you again. I have been so miserable for the last ten years! I love you. Nothing is like it was before. We are not those young kids anymore. I would never leave you again. I was planning to come to Denver." How could she make him believe that? She'd walk through fire to stay with Hunter. She had tried life without him and had only marked time until he'd reentered it. She was older and wiser. She'd cherish this second chance all her days.

"Remember I told you I had came close to marriage a couple of times? I didn't come that close. Nobody has ever come close to being you. I can live anywhere. I want to live where you live, and despite your offer of coming to Denver, I believe this is the best plan. Your mother needs all her family around her. She's not from Denver. I'm not from Denver, either. It's just a place where Trevor and I started our company. I can go anywhere, and I choose Seattle. Washington has as much to offer as Colorado, with the added bonus of the Pacific. But most importantly, it has you."

She wasn't convinced. It would make things easier if he moved to Seattle. Her mother could reestablish friendships. They'd be near family and be familiar with the city. But it was all one-sided.

"If I move to Denver, you'd know I'm choosing you," she said.

Hunter cupped Heather's face, brushing his fingers lightly against her cheeks.

"But that's it, Heather. I don't want you to choose anyone over anyone else. I want you to have both me and your mother. We'll get a big place and each have our own privacy. But there's enough love to go around. We can make it work, sweetheart. Trust me on this."

"I do trust you. I love you so much," she said. "I always have."

He kissed her. "Then it's a deal?"

Heather nodded, her eyes shining with happiness.

She and Hunter could go hiking, and make love beneath the tall trees, beside the splashing streams, under the star-studded canopy of the high mountain country. She'd have those babies she wanted, and her mother would relish being a grandmother.

"I love you, Heather," he said, kissing her gently. "Marry me and live with me forever."

"Yes." She kissed him, sealing the vow with all in her.

"Guess I'll start on a wedding quilt," Amelia said

softly with a smile, but neither of the other two occupants in the room heard her. They were in a happy world
of their own at long last.

If you enjoyed what you just read,
then we've got an offer you can't resist!

Take 2 bestselling
love stories FREE!
Plus get a FREE surprise gift!

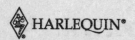
HARLEQUIN ROMANCE®

Coming Next Month

#3867 THEIR NEW-FOUND FAMILY Rebecca Winters

As a single mom, Rachel Marsden has always tried to do her best by her daughter. So when Natalie's long-lost father, Tris Monbrisson, shows up Rachel swallows her feelings. For the summer they will move to Tris's beautiful home in the mountains of Switzerland. But as she and Tris fall into the role of mother and father, the secrets of the past unravel....

#3868 STRICTLY BUSINESS Liz Fielding and Hannah Bernard (2 stories in 1 volume)

The Temp and the Tycoon by Liz Fielding—Her new boss, Jude Radcliff, is all work and no play...can Tallie persuade him to live life to the max—with her...?

The Fiancé Deal by Hannah Bernard—Louise Henderson is fighting for the same promotion as sexy lawyer David Tyler. She needs a fiancé fast—and David's the best man for the job!

#3869 MISTLETOE MARRIAGE Jessica Hart

For Sophie Beckwith, this Christmas means facing the ex who dumped her and then married her sister! Only one person can help: her best friend Bram. Bram used to be engaged to Sophie's sister, and now, determined to show the lovebirds that they've moved on, he's come up with a plan: he's proposed to Sophie!

#3870 THE SHOCK ENGAGEMENT by Ally Blake

Emma's colleagues and friends are delighted she is marrying the gorgeous and successful dot com millionaire Harry Buchanan—but their engagement is purely for convenience. Harry will get out of the excruciating "hunkiest male" competition and Emma will save her job. Only, Emma has dreamed of marrying Harry for years, and acting engaged is pure torture....

Office Gossip